"Kelly, I've never felt this way about anyone but you. I don't want to lose you."

"You won't lose me, Brad."

He searched her hazel eyes hopefully. "Do you mean . . ."

Kelly wanted to hear herself saying the words, "Yes, Brad, I'll go steady with you."

But she never got the chance. Before her lips could move, a shrill cry pierced the thick air of the gymnasium. Even the band stopped playing. A girl was screaming at the top of her voice.

"Help me! Please, help me!"

Brad stood on tiptoe, trying to see over the crowd. The dancers parted as the distraught girl pushed across the gym floor.

"Who is it?" Kelly asked.

"Liza," Brad replied. "And I think she's totally lost it."

Liza Brown burst through the crowd, stopping in front of Brad and Kelly. Black streaks of mascara flowed in the tears that striped her puffy face. Liza's whole body trembled as she tried to speak.

"Help me," she repeated. "Help *him*!"

Mr. Kingsley broke through the ring of onlookers who had surrounded them. "What's going on here?"

Liza grabbed his hands. "J-Jeremy," she stammered. "Jeremy is dead!"

This book also contains a preview of the next exciting book in the TERROR ACADEMY series by Nicholas Pine: *Spring Break*.

Berkley Books by Nicholas Pine

THE TERROR ACADEMY SERIES
LIGHTS OUT
STALKER
SIXTEEN CANDLES

SPRING BREAK
(Coming in September)

TERROR ACADEMY

SIXTEEN CANDLES

NICHOLAS PINE

B
BERKLEY BOOKS, NEW YORK

SIXTEEN CANDLES

A Berkley Book / published by arrangement with
the author

PRINTING HISTORY
Berkley edition / August 1993

All rights reserved.
Copyright © 1993 by C. A. Stokes.
Material excerpted from *Spring Break*
copyright © 1993 by C. A. Stokes.
This book may not be reproduced in whole or in part,
by mimeograph or any other means, without permission.
For information address: The Berkley Publishing Group,
200 Madison Avenue, New York, New York 10016.

ISBN: 0-425-13841-0

A BERKLEY BOOK ® TM 757,375
Berkley Books are published by The Berkley Publishing Group,
200 Madison Avenue, New York, New York 10016.
The name "BERKLEY" and the "B" logo
are trademarks belonging to Berkley Publishing Corporation.

PRINTED IN THE UNITED STATES OF AMERICA

10 9 8 7 6 5 4 3

This book is dedicated to
Liza R. and Karen B.,
best friends.

ONE

Kelly Langdon shifted nervously behind the creaking school desk, wishing that the bell would ring and free her from the school day and the droning voice of Mr. Forth, her English teacher. Her hazel eyes peered anxiously through thick glasses, fixing on the clock that hung over the chalkboard behind Mr. Forth's wooden desk. A few more ticks on the black and white clock face and Kelly could escape into the noise and confusion that always followed the final bell. Like a lot of juniors, Kelly found herself caught up in the frenzy that pervaded the close of the school year, the sense of urgency that had gripped Central Academy. The onset of summer had also enlivened the peaceful New England town of Port City, a bustling Atlantic village on the banks of the Tide Gate River.

In four short days, Kelly would be a senior. She would also be sixteen years old on the last day of classes, a circumstance that had been brought about by skipping the third grade. Being younger and smarter than most of the kids in her class had assured a lousy social life for the dumpy, over-weight girl from Pitney Docks, Port City's worst neighborhood. Even though she made straight A's (except for physical education her sophomore year), each school day was tedious for Kelly. She couldn't wait for summer vacation to arrive, even though she didn't really have any big plans like the other kids.

There were other tasks to attend to before Friday. Kelly wondered if she could cover it all in four days. She wasn't involved in the graduation ceremony or anything like that, but there were still a number of entries on her list of things to do. She took a deep breath and lowered her eyes to the blue-lined page of a composition notebook.

Study for finals. She was pretty much up-to-date but a review was in order for all of her subjects.

Computer Club banquet. Kelly, who served as secretary and treasurer of the club, had to make last-minute arrangements for their yearly banquet.

Money for class ring. Her Aunt Doris had not yet given her the money for the final payment on the ring, even though most of the other juniors had their rings by now.

Get yearbook signed. Because of money problems, she had received her yearbook two weeks late, but since she didn't really have many friends, she could get it done quickly.

Term paper for Mr. Forth. She drew a line through the entry because the paper had been finished for a week.

See Miss Monica. The appointment with her guidance counselor had been made a month ago, scheduled for tomorrow morning.

Kelly sighed, closing the notebook. It seemed like a lot to do in four days. The class ring worried her the most. What if her aunt could not come up with the balance? Doris Hendricks, her late mother's sister, did not earn a lot of money working in the kitchen at Port City Community Hospital. They were barely able to get by on what amounted to little more than minimum wage.

No class ring, Kelly thought.

Just another disappointment in a long line of disappointments that had followed the accidental deaths of her parents.

Kelly began to fan herself with the notebook as moisture formed on her pallid skin. Even if she had not been twenty-five pounds overweight, the high-necked blouse and plaid wool skirt would have been out of style and too warm for June. She couldn't get excited about a summer wardrobe, mainly because it meant combing the thrift shops with Aunt Doris, searching for shorts and tank tops that had been worn by someone else. At best, she'd get a new pair of cheap sneakers from K Mart.

The other girls were already wearing their warm-weather outfits. Kelly didn't care much about clothes. Fat girls weren't allowed to care.

They were filed away in some drawer with the other geeks who sat home on Saturday nights.

Kelly sighed with regret. They would probably have to spend the rest of the ring money on clothes. Things like that were always happening.

No class ring.

She'd just have to accept it. Live with it. Or without it. Kelly was used to being poor by now, accepting her condition with a dull sense of resignation.

The thick, horn-rimmed glasses—the cheapest frames possible, courtesy of Aunt Doris—slipped down Kelly's short nose. She had a pretty face, but no one noticed it behind the pop-bottle lenses. She pushed up the black frame and glanced at the clock again.

Why did the minutes have to tick so slowly when she had so much to do? Time would slip away as soon as she got on with her tasks. There wouldn't be enough hours in the day.

She kept fidgeting at her desk, rustling papers and making noise until she gradually realized that the room had grown quiet. Kelly lifted her head to see Mr. Forth glaring at her with his brown, beady eyes. His skinny, hawkish face was frozen forever in a perpetual state of scowling disapproval.

The entire class had turned in Kelly's direction, staring straight at her. Their faces were smirking, lips moving, voices whispering. All the students in the back row were laughing out loud, especially

Liza Brown, who relished the torment of a fat, unpopular girl from Pitney Docks.

Mr. Forth took a step toward the trembling Kelly, who always sat in the front row with the other studious types. "Your desk is squeaking under your weight, Kelly," he said in an unsympathetic tone. "You seem to be distracted today."

Kelly blushed and hung her head. A burning sensation rose in her chest and throat. She could hardly catch her breath in the stifling atmosphere of the classroom.

Mr. Forth, who was known for his sarcasm, continued in an accusatory way. "Miss Langdon, are you distracted?"

"More like disturbed!"

Liza Brown's haughty voice reverberated from the back row of desks. Liza tossed the mane of blond hair that fell to her shoulders. A couple of her cohorts giggled at the comment.

Mr. Forth's head jerked up as he focused on the rear of the classroom. "That's enough out of you."

Kelly sat there, wishing she could die. She took the humiliation with a red face. There was no real way for her to fight back. Fat girls weren't allowed to defend themselves.

Liza snickered despite the warning from the teacher. She was the exact opposite of Kelly—thin, gorgeous, and popular. Liza lived in Prescott Estates, dated Jeremy Rice, the most popular jock at Central and would be head cheerleader next year. Liza preferred fashion to studying, spending her free time on her hair and makeup in front of the mirror. Liza got through her classes by cheating and conning other students into doing her homework.

Mr. Forth focused on the chubby girl again. "Is there something wrong, Kelly?"

Kelly shook her head, fighting the urge to cry. *Why?* she kept thinking. Why is it always *me*? Can't they find someone else to pick on?

Mr. Forth threw up his hands. "I give up."

"What do you expect from Pitney Docks?" Liza whispered to a giggling ally.

Kelly cringed behind her desk, praying for the bell to ring. She hated being singled out for any reason, much less to have the others enjoy a laugh at the expense of the sweaty, dumpy girl with mousy brown hair and thrift-store clothes. Kelly had learned to ignore her tormentors for the most part, but she knew she'd never be completely immune to their barbs.

Mr. Forth cast a look of general hostility toward the entire class. "Need I remind you scholars that in order to receive a promotion from the junior to the senior class, I must have your term papers in my hand no later than this Thursday, same bat time, same bat channel."

A low groan rose from everyone but Kelly.

"Otherwise," Mr. Forth went on, "summer school looms on the horizon for the unprepared. Is that clear, Miss Langdon?" He focused on Kelly again.

She raised her head suddenly, meeting his gaze

with a hint of defiance in her eyes. "My paper is finished!" she said angrily.

Was that really *her* talking back to Central's meanest teacher?

Liza and the rest of the back row were silent for a moment.

Mr. Forth raised a thin eyebrow, ready to call her bluff. "Well, if that's so, maybe you'd like to turn it in now."

Kelly whipped out a cellophane folder that held five, crisp sheets of white paper. "Here," she said. "Take it."

Liza snorted contemptuously, trying to burst Kelly's balloon. "The fat nerd rules," she said.

The classroom erupted in mocking laughter. Kelly didn't hate them. She just wanted to be out of their reach.

Mr. Forth took the term paper and lifted it for the others to see. "Here's one person who will be promoted. Let this be a lesson to all of you. If more of you were this diligent in your—"

The bell intruded, clanging with the sound of deliverance. Kelly bolted from her desk, almost knocking Mr. Forth to the floor. She was in the hall before he could stop her.

Thank heavens, she thought. Now I can go home.

She trudged toward her locker, bumping through the hot, noisy corridor. Her head whirled with dizziness and she felt slightly feverish. Stopping in front of her locker door, she steadied herself against the wall of lockers.

Why did they always have to pick on anyone who was different?

What had she done to deserve this?

Nothing!

Her trembling fingers started to turn the wheel of the combination lock.

"Hi, Kell."

A reedy, dark-haired girl slumped back against the locker next to her.

Kelly startled and then took a deep breath. "You scared the heck out of me, Rachel!" She jerked open the locker door.

Rachel Warren blushed and turned her freckled face away from Kelly. "Sorry. I thought you'd see me coming."

Rachel was Kelly's best friend. They had known each other since elementary school. Rachel also lived in Pitney Docks. She was a skinny, intelligent girl with sad blue eyes and thin black hair. Her soda-straw figure had prompted Liza Brown to dub her Stick-girl, a cruel nickname. Like Kelly, Rachel also excelled in academics but she had little social life beyond the Computer Club, for which Rachel served as vice president.

She glanced back at Kelly again. "Bad day? You look frazzled."

Kelly sighed. "Mr. Forth was a jerk today."

Rachel laughed. "Today? He's always a jerk."

"I got back at him," Kelly offered.

"No way! How?"

A tiny smile parted her lips. "He was yelling about term papers and bang! I had mine already done. I handed it in right there. He was shocked!"

"You didn't!"

Kelly nodded. "It was great. It would have been greater but Liza and the scoff-patrol were cranked up."

Rachel grimaced and stuck out her tongue. "They can bite—"

"Rachel, Kelly. Hi!"

A husky boy with a crew cut had come out of the crowd to join them. He wore a bright red shirt and black polyester pants that barely dusted the tops of his wing-tipped shoes. His name was Marshall Butler and he was president of the Computer Club.

Rachel smiled at him. "Hi, Marshall."

Marshall nodded, but he did not look at Rachel. "Hi, Kelly. Gee, you look really nice today."

Yeah, Kelly thought, I don't sweat much for a fat girl who still dresses in winter clothes.

Everyone knew that Marshall had a crush on Kelly. He was always trying to ask her on a date. Kelly tolerated him but she didn't have any deep feelings for Marshall so she never spent time with him beyond the few social functions of the Computer Club.

"Marshall," Kelly said with a note of impatience in her voice. "How are you today?"

Before Marshall could reply, a derisive clamor rose in the hall.

"Look everybody," Liza Brown called, "Kelly has a boyfriend. Oh, Kelly, how could you take him away from me!"

Liza's little group of hangers-on enjoyed another good laugh as they moved away from Kelly.

Rachel frowned and shook her head. "Why does she have it in for you, Kelly?"

Kelly exhaled dejectedly. "I won't do her school-work for her. She asked me once and I refused."

The insult went over Marshall's head. He was actually smiling in his goofy way. If Liza thought he and Kelly should be together, maybe he had a chance with Kelly after all.

He grinned at Kelly. "Have you finished making the arrangements for the Computer Club banquet at the Ramada?"

She closed her locker door. "Yes. I just have to phone in the menu order. How's this sound? Chicken, potatoes, mixed vegetables, and Jell-O for dessert."

"Great. Kelly, I was wondering if you would be my date for the banquet. If you—"

She shook her head. "I can't, Marshall. I have other things to take care of that night. I mean, we will have twenty-five people there, including Mr. Tinker and his wife."

Mr. Tinker was the faculty sponsor for the club.

Marshall looked hurt. "But, Kell—"

She turned away from him. "I'm sorry, Marshall. I have to go home now. See ya."

Kelly moved down the hall, leaving a disappointed Marshall standing with a slack jaw in front of her locker.

Rachel fell in beside her. "You didn't have to blow him off like that. He always gets so upset when you turn him down, like it's always the first time you refused to go out with him."

Kelly grimaced and bit her lip. "I know. I feel bad about it. I mean, this banquet is such a big deal to him."

"It's a nerd banquet!" Rachel announced with sudden bitterness. "All the geeks who can't get into any other club join the Computer Club. Just like us."

"It's all we have," Kelly replied. "So we better try to enjoy it."

They exited the red brick structure to face the other two classroom buildings to the east. To the south were the gymnasium, the domed swimming pool that could be used year-round, the football stadium, and three baseball diamonds. Central Academy was a fairly new school, constructed in the boom of the Eighties. It was a public institution, Port City's only high school, but it maintained a high academic standard like many of the private schools in New England.

Kelly and Rachel turned south, toward Fair Common Park and Pitney Docks. The lower class neighborhood lay on the other side of the park, stretching from Taylor Street all the way to the gates of the shipyard. They could reach MacDonald Avenue, where Kelly and Rachel both lived, by going through the park and picking up Taylor there. They cut across campus, passing the gym and the domed structure.

When they reached Rockbury Lane, a side

street to the park, Rachel grabbed Kelly's arm. "Slow down. I have something to tell you."

Kelly came to a halt. "What's wrong?"

Rachel blushed again. "I was going to tell you in the hall but Marshall showed up."

Sweat poured from her face and Kelly felt her heart racing. Something else had gone wrong. The end to a perfectly horrid day.

"Jeremy Rice has been asking about you," Rachel said.

Kelly almost laughed. "About me?"

Rachel nodded. "Yes, today at lunch."

They started to walk again.

Kelly was inclined to think that such news could not be true. "Asking? What was he asking?"

"You know, if you were going out with anyone, did you have a boyfriend. Stuff like that."

"Really?" Kelly didn't know what to feel. Why would the most popular boy at Central be asking questions about her? Personal questions.

Rachel suddenly exclaimed, "Hey, I bet Jeremy is going to ask you out!"

Kelly scowled at her friend. "Impossible. I'm a fifteen-year-old geek girl who skipped a grade. He won't—"

"No," Rachel insisted. "That's why Liza is so mad at you. She made that remark about stealing her boyfriend."

Kelly lifted her eyes, gazing back down Rockbury Lane, watching the car that had turned onto the side street. It was a Buick Riviera, red and garish in the afternoon light. Kelly fixed her gaze on the approaching car, trying not to think about Jeremy Rice.

He was cute, tall, and muscular. Any girl would want to go out with him. Kelly had always pegged him as shallow, selfish. But maybe she was wrong, maybe he could judge someone by things other than physical appearance.

"You're almost sixteen!" Rachel kept on. "Maybe he has a crush on you. Kelly, this could be great."

Kelly was about to reply when the car stopped at the curb. It just sat there with the motor running. Rachel followed Kelly's eyes, turning to look at the vehicle.

"Who is it?" Rachel asked.

Kelly shook her head. "I don't know. Maybe he lives on this street."

The Buick just sat there.

"Why doesn't he turn off the motor?" Kelly said nervously. "Why isn't he getting out of the car?"

Rachel squinted at the front license plates. "It's a new car. Temporary tags. It's nobody."

Kelly sighed and shook her head. "What a day."

Rachel grabbed Kelly's arm and turned her back toward the park. "Come on, let's talk about Jeremy. What did you do to make him fall in love with you?"

"Rachel, I told you I—"

Kelly heard the revving of the engine as the driver put the car in gear.

They both glanced over their shoulders.

"Uh-oh," Rachel said.

Kelly felt the tightness returning to her chest and throat.

The Buick rolled slowly along Rockbury Lane.

The driver was following them.

TWO

Kelly and Rachel kept moving steadily toward the park where the car would not be able to follow them.

Rachel squeezed Kelly's arm. "He's after us. That psycho-killer is after us."

The red Buick idled slowly behind them, keeping its distance on the empty street.

Kelly glanced back over her shoulder. "Who is it?"

"Don't look," Rachel whispered. "Maybe he won't kill us if we don't look."

"Rachel, you're such a wimp."

Kelly eyed the creeping vehicle but she could not see the driver's face through the tinted windshield.

"Kelly, he's after us!"

Kelly turned forward, gazing toward the end of the street. The green of the park sloped upward beyond Rockbury Street, sprouting leafy elms and freshly trimmed maples. They were less than a half block away from the footpath that would take them to Pitney Docks.

"He's still there," Rachel said in a low voice.

Kelly could hear the whining engine. "This is ridiculous."

She felt buoyed after standing up to Mr. Forth.

"It's broad daylight," she went on. "This is a good neighborhood. We don't have anything to worry about. Ignore him."

Rachel stole a quick look at the red Buick. "Don't you watch the six o'clock news, Kelly? Psychos don't care what time of day it is. They work all shifts now."

Undeterred by Rachel's warning, Kelly stopped dead on the sidewalk. "I'm sick of this. I'm going to see what he wants."

"No—"

Kelly spun swiftly, facing the Buick. "All right, you jerk, why don't you open the window and tell us what you want!"

Rachel yelled, "Kell!"

Kelly took a step toward the Buick. The engine revved and the car lurched into the middle of the street, tires squealing as it pulled around them. It roared off toward the park, veering right onto Middle Road.

Kelly's heart pounded. She felt a sense of triumph as the car disappeared. Maybe it was time for her to start standing up to her tormentors. After all, she was going to be a senior. She was going to be *sixteen*!

"What a chicken," she said to Rachel. "Can't look me in the eye."

Her wide-eyed friend came up beside her. "Probably some pervert. Wow, you really scared him off."

Kelly sighed and turned back toward the park. "I'm sure it was one of Liza's cronies. They never give up."

"What creeps!"

"Did you see the driver?" Kelly asked.

"No, the windows were dark. I got the temporary tag number. Want to go to the police station?"

Kelly thought about it for a moment. "No. They'd probably say it's just some prank. Let it go. We'll be all right."

They started along Rockbury again, making for the park. Rachel was quiet, a little shaken. Kelly shook off the tingling sensation that came with every hazing. It was nothing new for the chubby girl from Pitney Docks. It seemed to come with the territory, the realm of the unpopular.

"Are you going to study for finals tonight?" Rachel asked.

"I think so," Kelly replied.

"Want to come over and have dinner?"

Kelly frowned, lowering her eyes to the ground, beset by yet another defeat. "I have to talk to Aunt Doris about my ring money."

Rachel didn't reply. She knew about Kelly's money woes. Her Aunt Doris was even poorer than Rachel's mother, who was divorced. At least Rachel's father sent child support to cover her stuff for school. Kelly's parents were dead, killed in a horrible accident up near Mount Adams, where their car went off a cliff six years ago.

"Kelly, I was talking to Mom. If you need the money for your ring, we could loan it to you."

Kelly shook her head. "No way."

"But you have to wear a class ring. You won't really be a senior without it."

Kelly was about to offer another protest, but the squealing sound from Middle Road made her turn toward the intersection.

The red car had returned. It was screeching down Middle Road, coming right in their direction. It swerved through the intersection, sliding onto Rockbury Lane.

"Run!" Rachel cried.

Kelly just stood there at the curb, frozen for a moment. Rachel tried to pull her away from the street but Kelly was too heavy for Rachel to budge her. The driver of the car slammed on the brakes. The Buick came to a stop right in front of Kelly.

"Help!" Rachel cried.

Kelly watched as the electric window dropped on the driver's side. "You!" she cried. "Have you gone crazy?"

Rachel focused on the handsome boy behind the wheel of the Buick. "Jeremy Rice. What are—"

Jeremy smiled, flashing perfect teeth and devastating green eyes. "Hey, Kelly, I thought that was you. Sorry, didn't mean to scare you."

Kelly's eyes narrowed. "You didn't have to—"

"Easy," Jeremy went on in a calm voice. "No

need to get wild on me, Langdon. I just thought—"

"Thought what?" Kelly challenged.

Jeremy shrugged and brushed an errant lock of thick brown hair from his forehead. "Uh, I was wondering if you'd like to go over to Tremont Mall with me, maybe go for pizza."

Kelly felt herself deflating. The invitation had caught her completely off guard. Why was Jeremy Rice asking her out for pizza?

"I can't," she said curtly.

Jeremy frowned. "Oh, come on."

Rachel tugged at Kelly's sleeve. "See, I told you. Go on."

Kelly blushed. "Uh, all right. Rachel and I will come with you."

Jeremy's smooth face tightened into a grimace. "Uh, I'd really like to take Rhonda with us—"

"Rachel," Kelly corrected.

"Whatever," he replied, gesturing to the back seat of the car. "Only, my dad says one person at a time in his new car. Tough luck, Rhonda."

Kelly shook her head. "Forget it, Jeremy. That's the lamest excuse I've ever heard."

Jeremy squinted at her. "Hey, don't be like that."

"Go with him," Rachel urged. "You'll score one for geeks everywhere."

"Yeah," Jeremy went on, smiling again. "I want to be alone with you, Kelly. Pizza. Yum. Come on, let's go to the mall."

"What about Liza?" Kelly challenged.

Jeremy waved at her, glancing away with a goofy smirk on his lips. "Ah, she's history."

Kelly stood there, waiting for the punch line. She glanced up and down Rockbury Lane, expecting to spot a bunch of Jeremy's good friends laughing heartily. Maybe he had lost a bet. Or maybe someone had dared him to ask her out as a fraternity club initiation. There had to be a catch. Guys like Jeremy didn't come after plump girls from the wrong side of town.

"I don't think so," Kelly told him.

"Aw, come on," Jeremy pleaded. "What'll it hurt to have a little pizza with me at the mall?"

Kelly was tempted to play it out, to try to guess the solution before it happened. What if Jeremy's offer was for real? A little voice told her to be careful.

Rachel pushed her toward the car. "It's only pizza."

Kelly knew she shouldn't go with Jeremy. After all, she wasn't sixteen until Friday. Her Aunt Doris had agreed to let her start dating then.

"Get in the car," Rachel whispered. "Or he's going to leave."

"Well?" Jeremy said.

She technically couldn't date until Friday. On the other hand, here was the most popular boy at Central, asking her out for pizza at the mall. It wasn't really a date, just an afterschool snack. And her aunt wouldn't be home for another two hours. She had time to play out Jeremy's little game.

It's a trap, she told herself.

On the other hand, how many chances like this would come her way?

Use caution.

But go!

Jeremy chortled and gave a defeated wave in the air. "Hey, if you don't want to—"

"No," Kelly heard herself saying. "I'll go."

"All right!" Rachel murmured.

Kelly stepped around the rear of the car and climbed in next to Jeremy on the passenger side. She closed the door and reclined in the plush seat. Rachel waved to her so Kelly waved back and smiled.

Jeremy winked out of the open window. "So long, Rochelle."

"Rachel!"

The Buick pulled away from the curb, tearing along Rockbury Lane.

Kelly saw the school again. She tried to remain cool but her body was tingling. Wasn't this what every girl dreamed of? Riding with a handsome boy in a fancy car.

She pinched herself. It wasn't a dream. Or a nightmare, like the awful vision she had of her parents' accident. She had never seen the car crash but she still dreamed about it sometimes.

Jeremy looked sideways at her with a strange, impatient expression. "So, how're you doing, Kelly?"

She shrugged. "About the same, I guess."

Jeremy's lips twisted into a dry smirk. "Hey,

take off those glasses for a sec. No, go on, it's all right."

Kelly removed the awful glasses from her blushing face. "There, is that what you wanted?" she asked curtly.

Jeremy nodded, running a hand over his thick dark hair. "You know, you aren't half bad. You got a cute face."

She quickly put the spectacles on again, looking away from him. "I really wish you wouldn't tease me."

"I'm not teasin', Kelly. I mean, you're a smart girl. A lot smarter'n me. Heck, I'm just a dumb jock."

She looked at him again. Why was he being so self-deprecating? Was he really trying to win her respect?

She relaxed some, attempting to maintain her composure. "I—I'm sorry, I—I've had a bad day."

"Aw, I have 'em all the time. Hey, let's listen to this new CD I bought yesterday. I think you'll like this."

Classical music filled the interior of the Buick.

"That's Bach," Kelly said. "My favorite. How did you know?"

Jeremy shrugged. "I looked it up in the yearbook, where they have all that stuff."

Kelly allowed herself to smile. "You did that for *me*?"

"Yeah, I been thinking that I oughta get a girl with some brains, you know, one I can talk to."

Could this really be happening?

Jeremy turned the Buick into the mall parking lot. He even ran around to open the door for Kelly. She was starting to enjoy their almost-date. Did the popular kids feel this happy all the time?

They started for the mall entrance. Jeremy walked beside her, casting cautious glances from side to side like he didn't want anyone to see him with Kelly. But she didn't notice. She was starting to believe the fantasy, to trust Cupid's arrow.

No wonder Liza had been so angry at her—Kelly *had* stolen her boyfriend!

They entered the air-conditioned comfort of the mall. Jeremy led her to the Pizza Emporium, a small restaurant in the food court. He ordered four slices and two large Cokes. They sat at a tiny, romantic table in the back corner of the food court.

"Eat up," Jeremy said.

Kelly found that she really wasn't hungry. She watched Jeremy, who didn't touch his pizza either. He kept gazing toward the other side of the mall, looking for someone or something.

"What is it?" Kelly asked, peering in the same direction.

"Er, nothing—"

Kelly thought she saw a flash of blond hair in the picture window of a clothing store. Was Liza stalking them? Why did Jeremy seem so distracted?

"Jeremy—"

He gestured at the paper plate. "Eat up, Kelly. I thought a girl your size could pack away a dozen slices."

"There it is," Kelly muttered.

The show of disrespect. Jeremy Rice couldn't help himself. He just didn't know how to act in polite company. Kelly was poor, but at least she had been raised to have manners.

She pushed the pizza away from her. "What do you really want, Jeremy?"

He let out a disgusted sigh. "Okay, Kelly, this is it. I'm having a party Saturday night, a pool party at my place. I wanted to invite you. Okay? Is that clear enough for you?"

Kelly suddenly felt bad for snapping at him. "A party?"

"Yeah, this would be a good opportunity for you to broaden your social horizons. All the cool kids will be there."

Kelly knew she could say yes. She would be sixteen on Friday. The party would be her first official date. How could Aunt Doris refuse to let her go out with Jeremy?

"All right," she replied. "I'll be happy to be your date, Jeremy."

She started to reach across the table to touch his hand.

Jeremy drew back as if a snake were about to strike him. "Uh, there's one thing, honey. You have to do something for me."

Kelly blushed, looking down at the table. "Jeremy, I'm not that kind of girl. I hope you don't think—"

He laughed nervously. "No, no, it's not that! No,

I want you to do something else. I mean, you're a smart girl, into computers and all that."

"Yes?"

He leaned forward, affecting a charm-filled expression. "Kelly, I need a big favor. I think you can help. See, I'm failing two courses, English and history—"

"I'll help you study for the finals," Kelly offered.

He sighed. "Uh, no, I want you to do it the easy way. I want you to change my grade for me."

"Change your grade?"

Jeremy grimaced. "Sure, you can hack into the school computer, can't you? Change everything. Who'll know?"

"I'll know!" Kelly snapped. "Forget it, Jeremy."

His upper lip curled into a sneer. "You can't do it! You don't know how! So get one of those computer wimps to do it."

The truth had finally revealed its harsh self to Kelly. Jeremy just wanted to use her. He really didn't care about her at all. How could she have thought any different?

"Come on," Jeremy urged, unwilling to relent. "It wouldn't take five minutes. You can invite all those nerds to my party. Just come through for me on this one thing. I mean, I don't wanna go to summer school. Bummer school!"

Kelly suddenly remembered that the club banquet was scheduled for Saturday night. She couldn't abandon her friends, real friends, not users like Jeremy. Even Marshall seemed like a knight in shining armor next to the handsome boy with the new car.

"You can do it, Kelly. If you—"

Kelly stood suddenly, almost knocking over the table.

Jeremy slid back in his chair. "Hey!"

She grabbed the large cup of soda and splashed it in Jeremy's face. "Change that, you jerk!"

Jeremy could not believe that he had been doused. "Just for that, you're walking home!"

"Gladly!"

Kelly grabbed her book bag and started to move through the maze of chairs and tables on the food court. She felt a hand grabbing her from behind. She turned, expecting to see Jeremy, but instead she got a surprise.

Liza clutched the shoulder of her blouse. "I told him you wouldn't do it, fat girl! I'm gonna make you pay for this. I—"

Kelly lost control. She lunged at Liza, pushing with all her strength. Liza tumbled backward, falling over the tables and chairs. For a moment, Kelly thought she had hurt the insensitive girl, but Liza scrambled quickly to her feet.

"You're gonna pay for this you tub of lard."

Jeremy came up beside her. "What a gross toad! I can't believe I was going to invite her to my party."

Kelly wheeled away from them, taking flight into the mall. She didn't care what they did to her. Nothing could make her feel any more humiliated.

"You hear me!" Liza screeched after her. "You're *dead* at Central!"

Jeremy grabbed her arm. "Let's split before security gets here!"

Kelly left the mall and headed for the bus stop in front of Montgomery Ward. Her body trembled from the confrontation in the food court. Had she really knocked Liza over those tables?

What a creep Jeremy was! Trying to use her like that. Let him go to summer school, she thought. It serves him right.

She watched for the bus until the red Buick turned in her direction. Her heart jumped. She didn't want Liza and Jeremy to see her. She faced the back of the rain shelter and prayed that they would go on by.

After a few moments, she glanced back at the parking lot. The red Buick had disappeared. What was she going to tell Rachel? The truth, the awful, ugly truth.

Jeremy had simply wanted to take advantage of her, to use her and then throw her away. Liza had been his accomplice. Now they were heading back to their spoiled world of wealth and privilege. A rich kid's world.

A world that would soon devour Kelly.

THREE

Her sixteenth birthday!

Kelly could not believe that the moment had finally arrived. At last, she would be old enough to get her driver's license. And her Aunt Doris would let her start dating, an agreement they had reached on her thirteenth birthday. Everything was going to be different now.

"Sixteen," she said, trying it on for size. "I'm sixteen!"

Kelly found herself on the sidewalk in front of her aunt's old house. She had gotten there so quickly. Her head whirled in a daze. Why did everything seem so strange? Was this what being sixteen did to a girl?

"I'm home!"

Rushing up the stone walk, she took the steep, narrow steps two at a time. She hesitated at the front door. She couldn't find her key, but it didn't matter. The door was already open.

"Aunt Doris?"

She peered into the house. It seemed so empty and barren. Wasn't she supposed to have a sweet sixteen party with cake and presents?

Kelly entered the dim foyer, listening for sounds of movement in the darkness. She called for her aunt again. No reply. The house was deathly still and silent.

It was her sixteenth birthday.

Didn't anyone remember?

Kelly tried a light switch but the power had been cut off. She felt her way into the deserted room, reaching for the telephone. But the line was dead. She could not call out.

Kelly hung up the useless phone. "Okay, you can come out now!"

Still no reply.

"Hey, this isn't funny."

Something creaked in the deep recesses of the dwelling. Maybe there was a surprise party waiting for her. Or maybe there was something else inside the house waiting for her, something to avoid.

Her heart pounded and sweat formed on her upper lip. "All right, if you won't come out, then I'm leaving."

Silence.

"I mean it."

She started quickly for the front door, only it was closed now, locked.

"Kelly!"

She looked back over her shoulder.

"Happy Birthday, Kelly!"

The eerie, unfamiliar voice rolled down from the second story. Kelly peered toward the dark staircase. A warm, glowing light flickered just beyond the top step of the second floor landing.

Was this her party?

The voice came again.

"Sweet sixteen. And never been kissed! Are you ready to celebrate, Kelly?"

"Who's there?" she called in a frightened tone.

"Come, darling. Come for your sweet sixteen celebration."

Kelly could not resist the promise of a party. The spell of the dim light drew her toward the stairs. They were all waiting for her on the second floor, hiding, ready to jump out and yell, "Surprise."

"Party time," the voice told her.

"Yes," Kelly murmured. "My party."

When she stepped onto the landing, she studied the flickering light for a moment. Her eyes grew wide. A large, three-tiered birthday cake rolled toward her, decorated with sixteen candles.

Kelly counted them just to make sure. The circle of flame illuminated her innocent, happy expression. The cake looked so perfect.

"You can all come out now," she called to the shadows. "I want you to . . . No, don't—"

A black shape had crept into the light, hovering over the cake. Kelly could not see the face of the menacing figure. The intruder raised both hands in the air, waving bony fingers in the shadows.

"What are you doing to my cake?" Kelly cried.

The specter brought both hands down, smashing the knife dead center into Kelly's birthday cake.

Kelly could hear the intruder moving toward her, scuffling on the black landing. "No, stay away!"

But the shape kept coming, backing her toward the top stair.

"Sixteen candles," the eerie voice mocked. *"You aren't worthy of sixteen candles!"*

Kelly's feet hit the edge of the stairwell. She teetered there at the top, trying to keep her balance. But the evil demon was almost on her, its hot breath blowing on her face.

"No!"

"Sixteen candles, Kelly. You'll never see seventeen!"

Kelly cried out, lifting her arms to defend herself.

The intruder lurched at her. "Never!"

Kelly lost her balance, tripping into the pitch-black hollow of the stairwell. She felt herself falling into the dark pit. The chomping maw of death threatened to swallow her up. . . .

Kelly opened her hazel eyes to dull evening shadows, escaping the horrid dream. She sat up in her bed, gazing toward the light on the pink, thrift shop curtains that hung on both sides of her open window. A cool breeze stirred soothing drafts of air through her sparsely furnished bedroom. The days were growing longer, too long for Kelly.

A shiver spread through Kelly's thick body. She was back at her aunt's house in Pitney Docks. It wasn't her birthday. It was only a few hours after Liza and Jeremy had played their hateful trick.

Dropping her legs over the side of her bed, she put her feet on the worn hardwood floor. The whole day came back to her in one foul rush of merciless memory. All along, she had been expecting some juvenile trick from Jeremy. Even though she had doused him with soda and had pushed Liza to the ground, the charade had wounded her to the quick.

Why did it hurt her so badly? Because she had let her hopes soar too high. The fall was always painful. Girls like Kelly weren't allowed to soar.

The bus had taken her home from Tremont Mall, back to Pitney Docks and the run-down townhouse. Her aunt had not come home yet, so Kelly had run upstairs, flopping on her bed. She cried until she fell asleep.

The nightmare had come out of nowhere to waken her, to bring her back to the harsh sting of her real life. It was a new dream. In the past, she had been plagued by nightmares of her parents' untimely accident. Though she had not seen the car going off the cliff, the vision haunted her at least once a month, especially during periods of stress.

"Why do I even bother?" she said aloud.

She switched on the lamp that rested atop the secondhand night table next to her bed. The old clock on her wall told her it was past seven. She slid off the bed, moving to her bedroom door.

She had to see if her aunt was home and ask her for the rest of the money for her class ring. She couldn't be the only senior without a class ring on her finger.

The hallway was dark and drafty. Kelly listened for her aunt but the house was quiet. She slogged to the top of the landing, gazing down the hollow of the stairwell.

"Aunt Doris?"

No reply.

It was almost like her dream.

She started carefully down the stairs, holding the bannister in the shadows. Her aunt was never late. She was always home by six. Why hadn't she come home today?

"Aunt Doris?"

She was halfway down the stairs when she heard the scuffling. She saw the dark shape at the bottom of the staircase. Kelly drew back a step as the face lifted toward her. Suddenly the foyer light came on and her Aunt Doris was gazing up at her with a disapproving expression.

"You shouldn't walk around in the dark," Aunt Doris said in a gravelly voice. "You'll fall and break your neck as clumsy as you are."

Kelly sighed, almost wishing that the dream demon had appeared instead of her aunt. "I—I'm sorry. I took a nap. I just got up and I wanted to see if you were home yet. I need to—"

Aunt Doris shook her head. "I went out with a couple of the girls from work. We had a couple of drinks at the bar. Is that all right with you? The few moments of pleasure I get in this life."

Kelly knew better than to reply. Her aunt was in a bad mood, the usual state of her disposition. Kelly watched her move into the kitchen. She braced herself for the confrontation. She dreaded the result but she had to ask about the ring money, as well as her birthday party. She prayed that her aunt would be agreeable on both counts.

When Kelly came into the kitchen, the tall, slump-shouldered woman stood at the kitchen counter with a bottle of whiskey in hand. She sipped it from a jelly glass. Her aunt drank often, but she was not violent or abusive with Kelly—not physically anyway. A sharp tongue could sting as much as a slap to the face.

Kelly sat down at the table, waiting for the right moment.

Aunt Doris turned to face her. She was a gaunt woman with sunken cheeks and deep lines on her forehead. She was only a few years past fifty, but looked older, with few dark strands of hair amid the gray. She had never been a handsome woman like her sister, Lilah Hendricks, Kelly's mother. She still wore the white, food-stained uniform from the hospital.

"Did you find something to eat?" she asked Kelly.

"Er, no. I fell asleep."

Her aunt shrugged. "We'll order a pizza."

Pizza. How ironic. Kelly never wanted to eat pizza again after the incident at the mall. In fact, she didn't want to eat anything at all.

"Do you want pepperoni?"

Kelly shook her head. "No, I don't want any pizza."

"Well, if that's not good enough for you—"

"No, it's not that, Aunt Doris. I was wondering if we could just talk for a minute."

Her aunt sat down at the table, reeking of whiskey and cigarettes. "Hey, kid, I was thinking. How about having a couple of your friends over for your birthday on Friday night? You can invite that girl Rachel and your boyfriend, what's his name—Marshall? We'll have ice cream and cake."

The sudden kindness had caught Kelly off guard. "A party? Oh, sure. Uh, that would be nice."

Aunt Doris's pale face grew longer. "Is something wrong with that? I mean, don't you want your friends to come over?"

Kelly experienced a rush of guilt and shame. Aunt Doris did her best to take care of Kelly. She had never bailed out on her after Kelly's parents had died. Doris Hendricks had never married and Kelly somehow held herself responsible for that.

Who wanted to marry a homely woman with an orphan child?

"I do my best to keep you fed and clothed," her

aunt went on, slurring her words. "If that's not good enough for you—"

"No," Kelly pleaded in an apologetic tone, "it's just that—I was wondering if I could pick up my class ring before Friday. The balance is sixty dollars."

Aunt Doris sighed, a long, plaintive, impatient sigh that told Kelly to expect the worst. "Sixty dollars? Do you know how long I have to work to make sixty dollars?"

Kelly slumped in the wooden chair. "I know."

"I'm sorry, honey," Aunt Doris said in a more consoling voice. "I'm going to be short this month as it is. We'll have to hit the thrift shops to find you a few things for summer."

Tears began to form in Kelly's eyes. She knew her aunt could not help being poor. They were lucky to be making it, to be alive.

But it still hurt.

No class ring.

She would be the only student without one.

"I'll order that pizza," her aunt said.

The only one.

What more could a fat girl from Pitney Docks expect from her life?

When the pizza came, Kelly forced herself to eat a slice. She wasn't hungry but she didn't want to offend her aunt. After dinner, she went upstairs and took a shower. She decided to retire early, crying softly in the privacy of her room.

That night, she dreamed about her parents again. Her mother's pretty face loomed in front of her. Lilah Hendricks Langdon kept telling Kelly that everything would be all right. Then the car went off the cliff right in front of Kelly.

And when she awoke in a sweat, the alarm went off immediately, telling her it was time to get ready for school.

FOUR

"Kelly! Over here!"

Kelly was climbing the concrete steps to the main entrance of Central Academy when she heard the meek voice behind her. She stopped in the middle of the stairs, looking back over her shoulder. Rachel was hurrying toward her, waving her hand in the cool morning air. Kelly waited for her to catch up.

The day had not grown hot so Kelly had not yet begun to sweat in the heavy fabric of the gray dress. Aunt Doris had not given her much hope for a spiffy, warm-weather collection. With her unfortunate situation, an unbearable summer vacation loomed in the distance. That fact was almost a certainty.

Rachel started up the steps. Her slender frame was hidden in a loose-fitting T-shirt. She gazed at Kelly with eager curiosity. In her avid state of anticipation, Rachel wanted to know all the details of Kelly's pizza date with Jeremy Rice.

"How'd it go? Did he—"

Rachel stammered in midsentence. Kelly didn't have to tell her how the date went. The gloomy expression on her face said everything.

"How bad was it?" Rachel asked.

Kelly shook her head, exhaling. "The worst."

"No!"

"He wanted me to change his grades on the computer so he wouldn't have to go to summer school."

Rachel made an awful face. "What a slime! He's such a jerk!"

Kelly's full lips tipped slightly into a wry grin. "I—I threw soda on him."

"No way!"

"Coca-Cola, the thirty-two ounce cup. Then I pushed Liza into some tables. She hit the floor on her skinny butt."

Rachel was awestruck. "You didn't! My hero!"

Kelly didn't smile for long. She still couldn't feel right about what she had done. The incident had brought her down to Liza and Jeremy's disgusting level. Civilized, intelligent people didn't have to behave like cave dwellers.

An expression of terror seized Rachel's thin face. "Kelly! They won't let it rest. Liza and Jeremy will get back at you one way or another."

Kelly turned back toward the front entrance. "I don't care, Rachel. I really don't. I have an appointment with Miss Monica in a couple of minutes. I have to get going." She trudged up the steps again.

Rachel waved to her. "See you at lunch."

But Kelly did not hear her best friend. Her head had grown light and dizzy. She dreaded the session with her new counselor, Miss Cheryl Monica. They had met only once for a couple of minutes when Kelly made the appointment. She really didn't know Kelly, she didn't care. Nobody cared about Kelly, except to promote her as the laughingstock of Central Academy.

Miss Monica looked up when Kelly appeared in the doorway of her office. A young, attractive woman with long brown hair, Cheryl Monica sat behind a large desk that was covered with papers. She smiled pleasantly, bidding Kelly to sit down with a cheerful voice.

Kelly twitched anxiously in the wooden chair, unable to get comfortable. She wasn't sure what to expect from Miss Monica. Her other counselors had always left her alone because she made good grades. She just wanted the meeting to be over so she could get on with her miserable existence. There were still plenty of students at Central who hadn't laughed at her yet.

Miss Monica's kind brown eyes perused the text of Kelly's school record, "Straight A's this year," she said admiringly. "You're doing well. If you hadn't gotten that 'C' in phys ed your sophomore year, you might have had a shot at class valedictorian."

Kelly lowered her eyes to the floor. "I was never good at phys ed. I sort of hated it."

Miss Monica chuckled. "So did I."

Kelly glanced up at the hint of sympathy in Miss Monica's voice. "Really? You hated gym?"

"I was a total klutz. When we studied archery, I almost took out the teacher. Thank God I missed."

Kelly couldn't help but smile at her counselor's sense of humor.

"I was like you, Kelly. I skipped a grade. I was always younger than everyone else. I know the age difference creates problems that aren't there for the other kids."

Kelly felt a surge of hope. Did Miss Monica really understand?

"You live with your aunt?"

"Yes."

"Everything okay at home?"

Kelly shrugged. "I guess."

Miss Monica looked straight into her eyes. "Are you sure?"

Kelly sighed, wanting to open up without being overcome by emotion. "We—we have money problems sometimes. You know—"

"I'm afraid I do," Miss Monica replied. "We weren't exactly rich when I was growing up. I'm still paying off my college loans."

Kelly was silent for a moment as Miss Monica looked over her record one more time. She liked this brown-haired woman. No counselor had ever seemed to take a real interest before. They all thought Kelly was a genius who had no problems as long as she did well in her classes.

Miss Monica closed the folder and set it on her desk. "Kelly, you're a smart girl, but I think you need experience in other areas. What are your plans for the summer?"

"Uh, nothing really."

Miss Monica leaned forward, folding her hands together. "You need a break, Kelly. And I'm going to see that you get it. How would you like a job for the summer?"

Kelly's hazel eyes widened behind the thick lenses. "A job?"

"Yes, right here at Central. We're running a community outreach program from June until the end of August. It's going to be a busy time. We're offering arts and crafts, exercise programs, tutoring sessions for summer school students, first aid classes. You'll be lifeguard certified and you'll have to help with equipment. There'll even be college-prep seminars for advanced students like yourself."

Kelly could not believe what she was hearing. Was this another mocking dream that wouldn't come true? Or maybe some trick designed by Liza and Jeremy.

"You'll barely have a moment of free time during the day," Miss Monica went on. "People of all ages will be participating. The pay is seven-fifty an hour. There might be some overtime. I think I can fix it where they won't take out any taxes, providing that you didn't make too much money last year."

Kelly laughed. "I didn't make any money last year." Her aunt wouldn't sign the papers for the working permit, so she could never get a job.

"Of course, the school will provide you with uniform clothes, shorts, golf shirt, and running shoes. You'll have to provide the socks yourself."

Kelly hung her head. "Gee, I don't know—"

Miss Monica frowned at her. "What's wrong?"

"I—it sounds good. But I—I don't know if I can handle it. I've never had a job before. I don't have much experience."

"Well, you're in the Computer Club and they will need someone who can work a desktop."

Kelly leaned back in the chair, pondering. "Wow, a job. It sounds like a good one, too. I don't know if my aunt will sign the work permit."

"You don't need a permit when you're sixteen," Miss Monica replied.

"But I'm not—"

"You will be on Friday. You don't start the job until Monday."

"That's right!"

"Kelly, do you know how many kids would jump at an opportunity like this?"

Kelly nodded, wondering what her aunt would say. She hadn't allowed Kelly to work the previous summer. As soon as Kelly turned sixteen, she wouldn't need her aunt's permission. And how could her aunt complain if Kelly was earning her own money?

They were going to give her new clothes. And her class ring! She'd be able to pay for it now. How could her aunt say no?

Miss Monica seemed disappointed. "Of course, if you don't want to take the job—"

"No!"

"You don't want the job? Is that what you're saying?"

Kelly blushed. "No, I mean—yes. I'll take it."

"Great. I'll tell Coach Sikes that you'll be there at eight o'clock Monday morning. You can take care of the paperwork then."

"Uh, I don't have a driver's license."

Miss Monica shrugged. "Don't worry about it. Maybe you can sneak in driver's education. They're offering it in June." She picked up the phone to make the arrangements.

Kelly sat there, a bit stunned. How happy should she feel? She had never been one to expect the breaks to fall in her direction. She kept waiting for the bomb to drop.

Miss Monica hung up the phone. "It's all set. Your official title will be Recreational Assistant."

She had a title. A smile spread over Kelly's face. Could this really be happening to *her*?

"What's the matter, Kelly?"

"Uh, nothing. I—I just wondered why you're doing this for me."

Miss Monica smiled. "It's my job. Don't let me down."

"I won't."

Kelly remained in the chair, basking in her good fortune.

"Is there something else you wanted to talk about?" Miss Monica added.

"Er, no—"

"Then you can go. It should be time for the first bell."

Kelly got up, heading for the door in a trance.

"Kelly?"

She looked back over her shoulder. "Yes, Miss Monica?"

"If I don't see you before Friday, Happy Birthday."

Kelly was almost ready to burst with joy. "Thank you, Miss Monica. Thank you for everything!"

She flew down the hall, looking for Rachel. Kelly couldn't wait to share the good news. A job—with great pay! She could empty her closet of all the hand-me-downs purchased at church bazaars and thrift shops.

Her smile disappeared quickly when she saw Jeremy and Liza lurking in the halls. They cast hateful looks in her direction, muttering something that Kelly could not hear. Liza even made a nasty gesture with her hand.

Kelly moved on past them. They wanted to make her feel bad, but she wasn't going to let them ruin her day. To heck with the snobs and the jerks. Kelly had a right to be happy.

She had a job.

Her summer was looking better.

There'd be enough money for her class ring.

And on Friday, she'd be turning sixteen years old, the most important birthday of her life.

Things would be different now—in ways that Kelly could never imagine.

• • •

After the last bell on Friday afternoon, Kelly stood at her locker, scanning the entries on her "to do" list. All but one entry had been crossed off. Finals were over. The Computer Club banquet was set for Saturday at the Ramada. Her year-book had been signed by Rachel, Marshall, Miss Monica, and a few others. And finally, she had arranged to make the final payment on her class ring after she drew her first paycheck from her new job.

Only a single task remained: *Tell Aunt Doris about job!*

Somehow, Kelly had not found the right moment to approach her aunt. She was afraid Doris Hendricks would go mental. She had always been so strict.

Kelly planned to stand up to her aunt if the response was negative. She was sixteen now, this very day! She had a right to make certain decisions for herself. And she needed the money desperately.

"There she is, the fat phantom of Pitney Docks!"

Liza Brown's familiar tone penetrated the joyous confusion in the hall. Chaos always descended after the last bell. How had Liza even found her in the crowded corridor?

Kelly tensed, glancing sideways in the direction of the insult. A flowing mane of bleached blond hair bounced toward her. Jeremy walked beside Liza, holding her hand. They glared at Kelly. She glared back defiantly.

Jeremy snarled at her. "Thanks a lot, fatso. Because of you, I have to go to bummer school."

"Yeah," Liza rejoined. "Thanks a lot, Miss Gland-problem. You're going to pay for this one."

Undaunted, Kelly stuck out her tongue. "Hey, Jeremy. Want another Coke Classic?"

Jeremy flushed and waved her off. "Get outta here!"

Liza's jaw dropped. "You buffalo butt!"

"Bleached blond bimbo!" Kelly replied.

She wasn't afraid of them anymore and they knew it.

Liza dragged Jeremy down the hall.

Kelly finished cleaning out her locker and then slammed the door.

"They can't touch me!"

She was a senior now.

Sixteen legal years old.

Kelly glanced suddenly up and down the hall. Where was Rachel? They had to celebrate. A girl turned sixteen only once in a lifetime.

For a moment, she wished her parents were there to share the day. Were they looking down at her from some heavenly cloud in the great beyond? She wondered if they would be proud of her.

Kelly started home, keeping an eye open for Rachel. They hadn't made any real plans. Kelly had just assumed they would get together. She hoped Rachel hadn't forgotten.

Maybe she's picking out a great present for me, Kelly thought.

She ambled down Rockbury with her head in

the clouds. Fair Common Park was shining green,
alive with birds in the elms and maples. A warm
breeze stirred the air, carrying the sound of a
tugboat horn from the Tide Gate River. It was a
fabulous day, the best day of her entire life. She
didn't need some stupid sweet sixteen party with
a bunch of phony friends. That kind of stuff was
for spoiled snobs like Liza Brown.

Kelly walked to the other side of the park,
entering Pitney Docks. She turned onto MacDonald Avenue, peering at Rachel's house. She
knocked but no one was home, so she walked on to
her aunt's place.

As she approached the run-down townhouse,
Kelly saw that the front door had been left open.
She took a few steps up the stone walk, hesitating
as she gazed at the door. It was so similar to her
dream it was creepy. The door had been open in
her nightmare.

Why was it open now?

Her aunt didn't come home from work for another couple of hours. Maybe one of them had left
the door open that morning. Kelly drew closer,
listening for sounds of life.

"Hello?"

Peering through the screen door, her eyes
scanned the inner shadows. What if someone had
broken in? Maybe she should go to a neighbor's
house and call her aunt at work.

"Anyone home?"

She was about to turn away when a dim light
began to glow in the foyer. It was just like her

dream. She looked closer to see that the light was actually emanating from the kitchen.

"Who's there?"

So eerie, so similar to her dream. She couldn't go into the house. It was too spooky.

"Kelly?"

Her aunt's voice reverberated through the old structure.

Kelly opened the screen door. "Aunt Doris?"

"I'm in the kitchen, honey. I got sick at work, so I took a half day off. Would you come and help me?"

Great, Kelly thought. She's found a way to ruin my birthday by getting sick. I should have known.

But when she appeared at the archway of the kitchen, Kelly did not see her aunt. Her eyes focused on the center of the kitchen table. Sixteen birthday candles burned atop a white, one-layer cake. HAPPY BIRTHDAY had been written across the cake in red icing. Pink roses formed a clump where Kelly's name should have been.

"Surprise!"

Rachel jumped out of the broom closet.

Aunt Doris and Marshall had been hiding behind the table.

Kelly was flabbergasted. A cake! The candles burned brightly. And there were gifts on the table, glimmering foil packages and flowered boxes.

Rachel gave her a hug. "Happy Birthday. Your aunt planned it all!"

Marshall pointed to a red package. "That's from me. Open it first."

Aunt Doris shook her finger at him. "No. We have to eat ice cream and cake before we open gifts."

Kelly fought back the happy tears. "Oh, thank you. It's all so perfect."

"Make a wish," Aunt Doris said. "And blow out the candles."

Kelly thought all her wishes had come true. She bent over and blew out the candles in one breath. Then she sat down at the table with her guests.

Aunt Doris served ice cream and cake. She was dressed in her new Sunday outfit, a gray suit and white blouse. Her stringy hair had actually been combed for the occasion. She almost seemed pleasant to Kelly.

Aunt Doris sat next to her. "I'm sorry your name wasn't on the cake, Kelly. The bakery gave me a special price if I'd take the one that hadn't been picked up on time. There was another name where the roses are now."

Kelly smiled at her aunt. "It's all right. Everything is just great."

· Marshall winked at Kelly. "Time to open presents."

"Mine first!" Rachel insisted.

Aunt Doris frowned a little. "The ice cream and cake were my gift. I'm sorry I couldn't afford anything more."

Kelly didn't mind. She opened Rachel's gift. It was a thin, silk scarf in baby blue, Kelly's favorite color.

"Now mine," Marshall insisted.

"Don't bust a socket," Rachel warned.

Kelly opened the red foil box to find a new sports watch, complete with alarm timer and stopwatch. "Oh, Marshall, this is too much."

He blushed and waved at her, his affection a little too obvious. "Aw, I got it free with my new computer."

Rachel admired the high-tech timepiece. "Wow, Kelly, that'll come in handy when you start your new job!"

Aunt Doris glanced up with a hostile expression on her lined face. "Job? You didn't tell me about any job."

Kelly stiffened, holding back the rush of nerves. "Uh, I've been meaning to tell you. I've got a job at the school this summer, I'm going to be helping at the recreation center on the Central campus."

Aunt Doris grimaced and stared up at the ceiling. "Yeah? What're they going to pay you?"

Kelly found that her mouth had gone dry. "Uh, minimum wage," she lied, not wanting to show up her aunt.

Doris Hendricks sighed and nodded. "Same as me," she said, relaxing.

"I'm sorry I didn't tell you sooner," Kelly said, "but I—"

"It's all right," her aunt replied. "It's time you started working. And it's only for the summer. Your grades won't suffer."

"I can also start dating," Kelly reminded her.

"All *right*!" Marshall said, enthusiastically.

Aunt Doris was not smiling, but she agreed to

stick by their bargain. "You're sixteen now, Kelly. I can't protect you forever. You can do whatever you want from now on, providing you keep up your grades."

Kelly had not expected her aunt to give in so easily. "Thanks," she said, giving Aunt Doris a little hug.

Aunt Doris quickly scampered to her feet. "Hey, we haven't sung the song for the birthday girl!"

"I'm ready," Marshall said.

Rachel laughed nervously, thankful that everything had turned out all right between Kelly and her aunt. "Happy sixteenth, Kell. You're a senior now."

They began to sing off key. Kelly was floating on air, lounging in the clouds. Everything had worked out so wonderfully.

For the first time in her life, the plump girl from Pitney Docks thought anything was possible.

FIVE

Three months later

Kelly's heart pounded, her chest ached for air, her legs throbbed and burned. She kept her arms pumping, propelling herself forward on the oval track that ringed the football field of Central Stadium. The soles of her running shoes beat a steady rhythm on the surface of the inside lane. She was trying to complete the eighth and final lap. It was the first time all summer that she had tried to run two miles. She had been working up to it gradually, but now that it was almost over, Kelly wasn't sure she would last the distance.

Her cumbersome glasses slipped on her nose. She pushed them back up. The thick lenses dripped with perspiration. Kelly could barely see two feet in front of her, but she persevered, rounding the wide arc of the final turn. Victory was right there in front of her. All she had to do was take it.

For a moment, she thought she might collapse. But when she saw the finish line ahead of her through the fog on her glasses, a sudden, unexpected surge of energy filled her. Kelly found herself flying across the line in a final sprint. She raised her hands in the moment of triumph. She had really done it. Two miles!

Stumbling into a walk, she put her hands on her hips and tried to catch her breath. Kelly felt like she was floating. Was she about to faint? No, the energy stayed with her.

"Way to go, Kelly!"

She heard applause coming from the stadium bleachers. With her glasses blurred, she could see a figure descending down the center aisle between the fifty yard line seats. She recognized the voice of Coach Evelyn Sikes, the lean, blond, blue-eyed woman who had been her boss all summer at the recreation center.

Kelly had been a valuable asset to the community program at Central. The job had kept her quite busy. It had also allowed her to save almost two thousand dollars, even after she had helped her aunt with some of the household expenses.

"Did you run two miles?" Coach Sikes asked.

Kelly nodded. "First time," she replied, still gasping.

"You should think about running track for Central this year, Kelly. But I think you'd be a better sprinter than a distance runner. You're pretty fast on your feet."

Kelly blushed, shaking her head. "Oh, I could never run track. I'm not good enough."

Coach Sikes shrugged. "Well, think about it

anyway. You know my husband coaches at Rochester. I'd love to see our track team take them next year. He'd be so jealous."

Kelly took a deep breath, wiping her forehead. The afternoon was warm and sunny. A breeze stirred from the ocean to the east, fanning Port City with a hint of autumn. It was the end of a working day for Kelly, almost the end of the job. She had one week left before classes began.

"Have you started to enjoy exercising?" Coach Sikes asked.

Kelly nodded. "Yes, ma'am."

She had taken up running to supplement her low-impact aerobics class. The exercise made her feel better, but she knew she was still fat. She would always be fat.

"I need the keys to the minivan," Coach Sikes said. "Do you have them?"

Kelly ducked her head and her face turned pink. "Yes, I do—I—sorry."

She had taken driver's education in June, so she had her license now. Several times she had transported groups from the community center to activities throughout New England. She had become a good driver.

Reaching into the pocket of her baggy shorts, she handed the keys to Coach Sikes. "I'm sorry, I forgot I had them."

Coach Sikes took the ring of keys from Kelly's hand. "It's all right. I need the minivan for the senior citizens' bowling trip tomorrow."

"What time are we leaving?" Kelly asked.

"Uh, I thought I'd put you in charge tomorrow while we're gone," Coach Sikes replied. "It shouldn't be too busy for a Saturday."

Kelly frowned. "Me? In charge?"

Coach Sikes shrugged. "Why not? You know the routine. Just check out the equipment and keep a lid on the eight-year-olds."

"I don't know—"

"I trust you, Kelly. You've done a good job, especially the way you organized the computer files and the equipment inventory. We're going to save a lot of money this year. Thanks to your cross-referencing, we've been able to update the membership list and we found tutors for the learning center. You should be proud of yourself."

Kelly removed her glasses for a good cleaning. "It wasn't really that much. Anyone could have done it."

"Don't underrate yourself, Kelly. You've come a long way. Remember when you could barely make it around the track once. Now you can do eight laps. I'd call that progress."

It doesn't matter, Kelly thought. I'm still fat.

She remembered the physical examination her first day on the job. The school nurse had asked her to step up on the scale. She had weighed one hundred forty-eight pounds, too much for her five-foot five-inch frame. It had been a humiliating experience.

Coach Sikes studied the efficient but moody girl with the thick glasses. She knew Kelly lacked one thing—confidence in herself. Maybe it was time to give Kelly a boost, a kick in the seat. After all, August was almost gone. Soon school would be starting. Somebody had to help Kelly. She sure wasn't going to get any encouragement at home.

"Are you busy now, Kelly?"

"No, ma'am. Why?"

Coach Sikes stepped down onto to the track. "Come on, I want to show you something."

Kelly followed Mrs. Sikes into the weight room under the stadium. The football team had been working out all summer but the place was empty on this Friday afternoon. Kelly didn't like weight lifting, so she stuck to aerobics, running, and the occasional swim in the Central pool.

Coach Sikes navigated her way between the rows of weight machines, moving toward the back wall with Kelly behind her. "Are you taking those vitamins the school nurse gave you, Kelly?"

Kelly nodded. She had been cooking for herself at home, avoiding the fats and sugary foods that Aunt Doris brought home for dinner. The good diet of fish and vegetables had made her feel better, but she was still fat.

If only she wasn't such a blimp!

Coach Sikes stopped in front of a doctor's scale. "Step up," she told Kelly. "Let's see what you weigh."

Kelly blushed and lowered her eyes. She did not want to weigh herself. The result was always disappointing, humiliating.

"I'd rather not."

"Go on," Mrs. Sikes insisted.

Kelly sighed and stepped onto the scale. She moved the indicator which kept going down. The bar leveled off at one-nineteen.

Coach Sikes stepped back. "There, you see. You have made progress. I could tell you had lost weight."

Kelly pushed up her glasses, squinting at the indicator. "One-nineteen. That can't be right."

"The scale was checked yesterday morning by the team physician. It's right on the money."

Kelly frowned with disbelief, stepping off the scale. "Twenty-nine pounds. I've lost that much? I hope I'm not sick or something."

"You aren't sick, Kelly, you're just not fat anymore."

"But I—I *feel* fat!"

Coach Sikes grinned at her. "Kelly, it's common for a girl to lose her baby fat when she gets older. You've been very active this summer."

"I don't know—"

"It's also common for someone who has lost weight to still feel like a fat person. But you have to face it, Kelly—you're in good shape."

Kelly turned toward the mirror on the wall of the weight room. She looked at herself objectively. Had she really lost that much weight? Why hadn't she noticed it along the way? The baggy shorts and loose shirt made her look bigger. Twenty-nine pounds. It was a miracle.

"You know, Kelly, you should try contact lenses. You shouldn't hide your face behind those glasses."

Kelly touched her smooth cheeks. "Contacts, huh? I never thought of that. Aren't they expensive?"

"No, not really. And they won't keep falling down like those glasses. You should consider it."

"Maybe I should."

"Just a thought."

Contacts. Why not? She had the money in the bank. What if her aunt did not approve? It didn't matter. She could spend her money as she pleased.

Coach Sikes looked at her watch. "Uh-oh, gotta go. It's my turn to cook dinner tonight. I'll see you tomorrow, bright and early."

"Yes, ma'am."

"Don't forget, you'll be in charge."

Kelly nodded tentatively. "I'll do my best."

"You'll be fine."

Coach Sikes started for the door.

"Mrs. Sikes?"

She turned back for a moment. "Yes, Kelly?"

"Thanks. Thanks for everything."

"You're quite welcome. And don't forget what I said about those contact lenses. I think you'll like them."

"Yes, ma'am."

Coach Sikes hurried out of the weight room.

Kelly turned to the mirror again. "Contacts?"

She took off her glasses and drew close enough to see her image reflected in the mirror. Would contact lenses really make a difference? She hated the cheap glasses her aunt had bought for her.

Was her face really thinner?

Had she really lost twenty-nine pounds?

How could she have changed so much in three months?

She touched her hair, which had grown longer. The shoulder-length tresses were thick and silky. The vitamins had really helped.

She had never felt so healthy in her whole life.

"You look great, babe. Now clear out so a man can get some work done. Hey, you hear me?"

Kelly spun quickly in the direction of the rude speaker. She could not see the boy clearly as he approached, but she recognized the voice. Jeremy Rice had come into the weight room. He was walking toward her with his patented jock swagger. Kelly had not seen him all summer.

"This part of the weight room is for the football squad, babe. Coach Brunner is letting me use the place at night because I'm behind in my training. I had to go to summer school."

And I'm the one to blame for that! Kelly thought.

What would Jeremy do now that he had her cornered? Did he still begrudge the incident in the mall? Would he try to take his revenge?

"Then I went out of town with my parents. They—hey, look at you."

He came closer, standing a few feet away. Kelly felt her back against the mirror. Where had he come from so suddenly? Had he been stalking her? She thought she had put all her troubles behind her but here he was, leering at her with his handsome face.

"Where'd you come from?" Jeremy asked, staring at her.

Kelly blushed. "What?"

Jeremy took another step toward her, almost getting in her face. "You must be a transfer student."

"No—"

He put his hand against the mirror and leaned in toward her. "Then why haven't I seen you before?"

He was close enough for her to glare into his eyes. "You *have* seen me."

Jeremy chortled. "No way. I'd remember you. Anybody ever tell you that you're a total fox?"

Kelly tried to move around him but he stepped to the side. "Get out of my way, Jeremy."

"Hey, how'd you know my name?"

"Quit playing games," Kelly replied. "Don't you remember our 'date'? We went for pizza at Tremont Mall."

"You gotta be kidding me."

Kelly slipped on her glasses. "Remember now?"

His face contorted into a dumb expression of surprise and awe. "Kelly? Kelly Langdon? Wow, you used to be a real—I mean, what happened to you?"

She mustered her strength and shoved past him, moving toward the door. "Get lost, Jeremy." She glanced back over her shoulder to make sure he wasn't following her.

"Kelly! It's you and me babe!"

No way, she thought, not in a million years.

"You're beautiful, Kelly. I mean it!"

What a creep to be teasing her like that!

"I'm in love," Jeremy called as he clutched his heart in a mocking gesture.

"Yeah," Kelly muttered under her breath. "With yourself!"

SIX

Kelly did not go straight home from Central Academy. She wandered up Rockbury Lane in the direction of the park. She vaguely recalled the day that Jeremy had scared her with his car. It seemed so long ago, the cruel circumstance of a completely different world.

Things have changed, she thought.

But how did she feel about all these changes?

She turned onto Middle Road, walking parallel with the park, heading for the center of town. Port City was alive and bustling on this splendid Friday. Music drifted from the bandshell in Fair Common Park; a band was warming up for a production of *My Fair Lady*. The sidewalk was crowded with people walking toward the show.

Kelly went against the flow, heading for Congress Street. She stopped in front of the Port City Vision Center. A sign advertised soft contact lenses for under a hundred dollars, including the

eye exam. Maybe she should take the advice given
her by Coach Sikes.

Removing her glasses, she squinted at her reflection in the glass of the shop window. Had
Jeremy really mistaken her for someone else, a
beautiful transfer student? Or was it simply his
twisted sense of humor?

I'll think about it, she told herself.

Putting on her spectacles, she moved away from
the window, continuing along Congress Street
toward Market Square. The window of a dress
shop sported new outfits for fall.

Twenty-nine pounds, she thought.

What size dress would she wear now? A six? She
had always been a size ten or a twelve. She'd
have to buy some new clothes for school. And this
time *nothing* would come from the thrift shop.

In Market Square, Kelly stopped at the Rock-
ingham Deli to buy a plain turkey sandwich on
wheat and a small dinner salad. She sat on a
bench in front of the deli, eating and thinking. She
was uncertain about so many things, but at the
same time, she felt a sense of exhilaration.

Twenty-nine pounds.

She wasn't a fat kid anymore.

Why hadn't she noticed the change?

Rising from the bench, she sprinted over to
Pleasant Street, entering Fair Common Park at
the northwest corner. She jogged to Pitney Docks,
running across MacDonald Avenue to the dilapi-
dated townhouse.

When she reached the top of the steps, she

stopped and gazed at the open front door. She flashed back for a moment to a dream she'd had a few months ago. But Kelly was no longer afraid. She heard North Church chiming six o'clock. It was time for her aunt to be home.

She opened the screen door. "Aunt Doris?"

"In the kitchen," came the reply.

Kelly found her aunt at the kitchen table. Doris Hendricks nibbled at a take-out dinner in a plastic foam container. "I brought you a fried seafood platter with french fries," she told Kelly.

Kelly had stopped eating fried foods as part of her fitness program. She also knew that the plastic foam was no good for the environment. But she did not want to hurt her aunt's feelings so she made an excuse.

"Thanks, Aunt Doris. I'll put it in the fridge for later. I'm not hungry right now."

She could throw it away on garbage day.

Aunt Doris glanced up at her. "You never eat anything I bring home. There's a whole box of doughnuts in there untouched."

Kelly shrugged, avoiding her aunt's accusing eyes. "I've been changing my diet. And exercising. I've lost twenty-nine pounds."

Her aunt looked at her dully. "Oh."

She went on eating, refusing to offer any support for the results of Kelly's hard work. She wasn't exactly mean, just indifferent. They had never been close, but now they lived like strangers in the same house. Kelly didn't depend on her aunt that much now that she had a little money in the bank. And Doris Hendricks didn't seem to care as long as Kelly stayed out of her way.

"There's a letter for you," Miss Hendricks said. "I think it's from Rachel. Came today."

Kelly picked up the peach-colored envelope from the table. The postmark was from Sebago Lake, Maine. Rachel had gone up to see her father around the beginning of July. Kelly missed her a lot.

"I'm going upstairs," Kelly said.

"Better eat something."

It was almost as if her aunt wanted Kelly to be overweight.

"I'll eat later."

"Suit yourself," Aunt Doris replied.

Kelly left the kitchen, hurrying up the stairs to her room. She sat on the bed, immediately opening the envelope. Rachel always wrote entertaining letters. This was her third communication since she had left Port City.

Dear Kell: Boring, boring, boring. Unless you like nightcrawlers. My dad loves to fish, as I told you. I finally caught a trout. He's so proud of me. I couldn't care less.

Kelly laughed at the thought of Rachel wrestling with a slimy trout.

I got a letter from Marshall. He's still in Indiana. He has a major crush on you and he thinks he might have a chance to go steady with you this year. Let him down easy.

"I'll try," Kelly said to herself.

Dad sprung a major thing on me Sunday. He

has a new girlfriend and she's really gross. I hate her.

At least you have a father, Kelly thought.

Will be home Saturday before Labor Day. Meet me at the bus around four. Don't be late! Love, Rachel.

Kelly read the letter again just for the fun of it. She missed her best friend. Kelly didn't have anyone to talk to while she was gone.

What would Rachel say when she saw that Kelly had slimmed down?

Kelly folded up the letter and put it in the top drawer of her dresser. She then removed a small jewelry box from the same drawer. Opening the box, she took out the gold, Central Academy senior ring. She put it on her hand and admired the class ring again. Kelly had not worn the ring all summer because she was working at the gym. She had been afraid that she would lose it or damage it somehow.

She decided to keep the ring on her finger for the rest of the night. After all, she was a senior now. Why shouldn't she wear it?

As she closed the drawer, her glasses slipped down her nose again.

Kelly peeled them off her face. "That's it! I'm going to do it."

She had to put on the glasses again to see. Moving to her bedroom door, she listened for her aunt, who was still downstairs. Kelly opened the door and crept into the hall, lifting the extension phone to her ear. She dialed the number for directory assistance.

"Yes, could you give me the number for the Port City Vision Center?"

She committed the number to memory. It was time to change. She didn't have to be a fat, nerdy girl anymore.

As she dialed the number, she hoped that the Vision Center was still open. It rang four times before someone picked up.

"Port City Vision Center, may I help you?"

"Yes," Kelly replied, smiling. "I'd like to make an appointment."

"For glasses?"

"No. For contact lenses. When can you fit me in?"

When Rachel Warren saw the sign that announced, PORT CITY, NEXT EXIT, she sighed and leaned back in the bus seat. She thought the bus was never going to get her home. It seemed like she had been away from Port City forever.

The summer in northern Maine had been unbearable for Rachel. No friends around, nothing to do but go fishing, having to deal with her father's new ditzy girlfriend. It had been worse than going to summer school.

Rachel hated the fact that her parents were no longer together. But there was nothing she could do. Except talk to Kelly about all the putrid things that had happened on her summer vacation.

The bus pulled off the interstate, rolling down

the ramp. Home at last, Rachel thought. School would be starting in four days. Her senior year. She tried to look forward to being in the twelfth grade, but a nagging sense of dread had come over her. It would probably be the same old story: the geeks from the computer squad watching all the popular kids having a good time.

The bus pulled into Market Square, stopping in front of the bank.

Rachel grabbed her nylon sports bag and moved down the aisle between the seats. She hoped Kelly would meet her. They had so much to talk about.

Much more than Rachel could imagine.

Kelly stood in front of Averill's Stationery Store, which served as a ticket office for the bus line. She watched the passengers as they unloaded, waiting for Rachel who was the last one off. Kelly smiled and waved, but Rachel did not seem to see her.

Rachel walked straight toward Kelly with the sports bag swinging from her shoulder. She stopped right in front of Kelly, dropping the bag to the ground for a moment. Rachel's head swung in every direction, as if she were looking for some-one.

Kelly shook her head. "Rachel! Over here!"

Rachel's face snapped in Kelly's direction. She regarded the slender, long-haired girl with the sparkling hazel eyes. Kelly had on her new uni-form from the job at school, a smaller, tighter-fitting pair of shorts, and a sleek new golf shirt.

"Rachel, what's wrong with you? Why are you looking at me like that?"

Rachel frowned. "Do I know you?"

"Rachel! It's me, Kelly! Don't you recognize me?"

Rachel's eyes widened in amazement. "Kelly!"

Kelly laughed. "I made a few changes while you were gone."

"I'll say." Rachel looked her over. "Where are your glasses?"

Kelly shrugged. "I got contacts. I've been wearing them since Thursday. They aren't bad. And they don't slip down like my glasses did."

"And your hair!"

"I let it grow long," Kelly replied. "And I lost twenty-nine pounds. Can you believe it? Jeremy didn't even recognize me the other day."

Rachel shook her head slowly. "Wow, I knew you had lost some weight before I left, but look at you. You're svelte!"

Kelly smiled modestly. "I wouldn't say *that*."

"You're wearing your class ring, too."

Kelly wiggled her fingers. "I decided to let go. I mean, school starts on Tuesday."

Rachel gave a short whistle. "Radical! The boys will be all over you. Can I have the leftovers?"

"Stop!" Kelly insisted cheerfully. "The boys won't be all over me."

"Don't bet against it." Rachel picked up her bag. "Come on, let's walk home. I have to see my Mom.

I want to make her feel guilty for sending me up to the boonies."

Kelly reached into the pocket of her shorts. "We don't have to walk. I have the minivan from school. Coach Sikes let me borrow it to give you a ride home. She's great."

Rachel was still stunned by the change in her best friend. "Kelly, you're so different. You're—you're beautiful."

"Stop!"

But Kelly had to admit to herself that she liked hearing the compliment from a friend. She could trust Rachel to tell the truth. The genuine look of surprise would not leave Rachel's thin face.

They walked over to Pleasant Street and climbed into the minivan. Kelly had the use of the vehicle for the rest of the day. They could go anywhere they wanted as long as she brought the minivan back to school by seven.

Kelly followed Pleasant Street to Middle Road, where she made a left turn for Pitney Docks.

Rachel shook her head again. "I still can't believe it, Kelly. I think it's the contacts. You know, you have really pretty eyes."

"You want to hear the best part?" Kelly replied. "I've saved nineteen hundred dollars."

"No way!"

Kelly nodded. "I'm drawing interest on my account."

Rachel gazed straight ahead. "Nineteen hundred. Then that's it. We have no choice."

"What—"

Rachel grinned at her best friend. "As soon as I check in with Mom, we're going shopping!"

"Try a little more eyeliner," Rachel said. "Yeah, that's it. Now the mascara."

Kelly looked at her face in the mirror on Rachel's vanity table. It was Labor Day. Central Academy would be opening its doors tomorrow. Kelly was in the process of sorting through all the things they had bought that weekend at the Labor Day sales. She was trying on the makeup at Rachel's because she didn't want her aunt to see her yet.

Kelly dabbed at her eyelashes with the mascara brush. "Are you sure I'm putting this on right? I mean, I'm not exactly like Liza Brown. I've never lived for cosmetics."

"You're doing fine," Rachel replied. "Use some more of that blush. The thick brush. On your cheeks."

Kelly added very little to the slight smudges of red. She didn't want to be able to write her name in the thickness of her makeup. She just wanted to look better.

Rachel shook her head. "Wow, it's not hard to see why Jeremy thought you were someone else. It's like magic."

Kelly put down the brush. "That's enough."

Rachel peered over Kelly's shoulder. "Now, shake your head."

"What?"

"Shake your head, like the fashion models do. Go for that wild look. Go on, you'll see."

Kelly reluctantly shook her head. When she gazed back into the mirror, she no longer recognized the beautiful girl who stared out from the glass. She really *was* gorgeous.

"Stand up," Rachel said, "for the full effect."

Kelly stood, turning in a slow circle. She wore tight-fitting, stone-washed jeans, a beige tank top, a string of ceramic beads around her neck and black, high-heeled patent-leather boots. She smiled when she caught a glimpse of herself in the full-length mirror on Rachel's door.

"Wow," Kelly said. "Is that me?"

"You look like Cindy Crawford," Rachel replied.

Kelly studied herself in minute detail. A warm sensation spread through her as she admired her new form. She tingled all over, the ugly duckling now transformed into a sixteen-year-old beauty.

"Liza is going to be so jealous," Rachel offered.

A vengeful smirk spread across Kelly's full lips. "Think so?"

Rachel also gazed into the mirror. "She *has* to be. When you go to school tomorrow, you'll be the best-looking girl in the senior class."

Kelly did not protest. Why should she deny her good looks? She had worked hard to get this way. Maybe she would be the new beauty of Central Academy.

Rachel frowned. "Uh-oh."

"What?" Kelly asked.

Rachel sighed. "I was just wondering what your

aunt is going to say when she sees you looking like this."

Kelly's throat tightened for a moment. Aunt Doris hadn't protested any of her self-improvement habits so far, besides the occasional comment that she should eat more. What would she do when she saw Kelly's new look?

Kelly planned to fight any resistance from her aunt. After all, she had earned the money for the make-over, the cosmetics, and the new clothes. Kelly could dress any way she wanted. It was her right.

She worried about her aunt's reaction until she went home that night. When she showed Doris Hendricks her new outfit, Kelly braced herself for the worst. But her aunt only nodded and went about her business as if she hadn't really noticed the change in her niece.

SEVEN

The next morning, Kelly left the house a half hour early, sprinting across the street to meet Rachel. They were both excited about the beginning of the school year. As they walked to Taylor Street, their pace quickened with each step. They were filled with anticipation, like two debutantes about to experience a coming-out cotillion.

"I wonder if anyone will notice me?" Kelly pondered aloud.

Rachel nodded. "They will, trust me."

Kelly looked great in the beige tank top and faded jeans. The high-heeled boots made her seem taller. Her brown hair shimmered in the September sunlight and the contact lenses gave a bright sparkle to her gold-flecked hazel eyes. If Rachel hadn't been so happy for her best friend, she might have been jealous.

"Do I have on too much makeup?" Kelly asked.

"No, it's perfect. Don't worry, you'll do fine."

As they started across Fair Common Park,

Kelly tried to fight off the butterflies that fluttered in her stomach. She wasn't sure she could play this new role convincingly. She had been fine during the summer, but this was different. She would be facing the entire student body. Would they accept her transformation?

When they reached the other side of the park, Kelly stopped, taking a deep breath. "I don't know if I can do this, Rachel."

"Kelly! Don't worry so much!"

"What if they laugh at me like they've always done?"

"They won't laugh. I promise."

All of a sudden, Kelly felt fat again. She knew firsthand about the cruelty of her classmates. She had been the object of their abuse for years. What if it happened all over again?

"Come on," Rachel urged. "It'll be all right."

Kelly sighed. "You're right. We can't miss school."

They crossed Middle Road, heading up Rockbury Lane. Central Academy loomed at the end of the street. Kelly did not feel like herself. It was almost as if she had assumed the identity of another person. The old Kelly had been fat and insecure, but at least she had been familiar and comfortable. What if she couldn't live up to this new character?

Kelly was about to confess her lack of confidence to Rachel when a horn blasted behind them. A car full of boys rolled slowly past them. Two boys hung out the back window, gawking at Kelly.

"Hey, foxy!"

"You and me, babe."

"Yo, good-looking, I need a date for homecoming!"

When Kelly and Rachel ignored them, they roared off down Rockbury, heading for the student parking lot.

"See," Rachel said. "They'll notice you. You haven't even made it to school yet and you're already causing a stir."

"They were yelling at *me*!"

A broad smile parted Kelly's red lips as her insecurities began to subside. The boys' behavior had been rude, obnoxious, and juvenile, but they had given Kelly an ego boost. She was starting to feel the power of her good looks, a power she had never known before.

As soon as she and Rachel hit the Central campus, heads began to turn in Kelly's direction. Boys gawked at the tall, slender girl whose long hair bounced on her shoulders. Girls gazed enviously at the striking beauty who would no doubt give them competition for the attention of their boyfriends.

Some of the comments reached Kelly's ears.

"Who the heck is that?"

"I don't know, but I hate her already."

"Wow, what an ultra-fox."

"Don't look at her!"

"I can't take my eyes off her. Hey, babe—"

Rachel grinned. "I told you so," she said under her breath.

They moved toward the front entrance of the school. As they approached the concrete steps, they saw Liza Brown and Jeremy Rice standing near the glass doors. Kelly immediately blushed. She saw the jealousy in Liza's haughty face when Jeremy smiled and winked at her.

"Uh-oh," Rachel whispered. "Trouble."

Kelly expected some sharp, hateful comment from Liza. But as they passed, the blond girl was silent for once. Liza just smirked and turned her nose in the air.

Jeremy kept staring, the slightest hint of lovesickness on his handsome face. "Hi, Kelly. Hi, Rhonda."

Liza nudged him in the stomach with her elbow, forcing a grunt of pain from Jeremy. They started to argue. Kelly wondered if Liza was still planning to get even with her for last June.

As they entered the building, Rachel laughed. "I don't believe it. You finally made Liza shut up."

Sweet victory! Kelly felt a rush through her entire being. The sensation almost lifted her from the floor.

As they wandered through the hall searching for their home rooms, a circle of kids began to form around Kelly. They all wanted to know her, including some of Liza's hangers-on. Everyone was eager to meet the "new" girl at Central, the hip-looking brunette goddess with the shining hazel eyes.

Who was she?

Where had she come from?

Why hadn't they seen her before?

Did she want to try out for the opening on the cheerleading squad?

In the hustle and bustle of Kelly's newfound popularity, Rachel was abruptly pushed to the edge of the crowd, shunted aside by the sudden interest in her best friend. She finally stopped, unable to keep up with Kelly. Rachel watched as the tide of well-wishers carried Kelly away from her.

"Hi, Rachel. Wow, who's that new girl?"

Marshall had stepped up next to Rachel. Like everyone else at Central, he was staring at Kelly. He had come back late from summer vacation and so was unaware of Kelly's transformation from frog to princess.

"Hi, Marshall," Rachel said with a sigh.

"Who is that girl? Wow, she's really cute."

Rachel glanced sideways at him. "It's Kelly."

"Kelly Langdon?"

Rachel nodded. "Believe it or not."

"No way. What happened?"

"She changed this summer," Rachel replied. "She lost weight and earned some money for new clothes."

"Where are her glasses?"

"She got contact lenses."

Marshall shook his head. "I'll never have a chance with her now, not if she looks like that."

Rachel had an unexpected flash of dread and sorrow. Kelly had always been a thoughtful and considerate person who avoided the shallowness embraced by some of their classmates. Now Kelly seemed to be right in the middle of all the things she had disliked.

"I've never seen anyone change so quickly," Marshall said.

Rachel exhaled. "I know, Marshall, I know. Let's just hope it's a change for the best."

Kelly sat on her bed, studying her smooth, pretty face in a round, hand-held mirror. Her return to Central had been a triumph. The past had vanished, all but forgetting the fat, nerdy girl who had been ridiculed by everyone. In her place stood the stunning, hazel-eyed beauty who was actually looking forward to her senior year. For the first time in her life, Kelly was riding a wave of popularity.

Her first school day had been fantastic, a fairy-tale story with a happy ending. She had made so many new acquaintances, guys and girls who had never even looked in her direction before. Now they all wanted to know her, to be her friend. Kelly realized that many of them were superficial, drawn to her because she was receiving so much attention from the other popular kids. But that seemed to be the price of being a winner.

Putting down the mirror, she leaned back on her pillows. What a day it had been! She wanted to relive it over and over in her head. So many wonderful things had happened.

Liza Brown had been deathly jealous of Kelly's new image. Liza was no longer the most beautiful girl in school. After only one day of classes, there were rumblings that Kelly had a chance to beat out Liza for homecoming queen. Could it really be possible?

Jeremy Rice was another story. He had tried to get close to Kelly all day. He followed her in the hall, stared at her in history class. He had even attempted to sit next to her at lunch, at least until Liza intervened, whisking Jeremy away to another table. Kelly relished the fact that she was driving Jeremy crazy. He really seemed to be in love with her.

But there were a lot of other boys for Kelly to choose from. They had swarmed around her like bees to a fall flower. Kelly really didn't care for most of them, especially the jocks who were obnoxious and pushy like Jeremy. Nor was she drawn to the cool, smooth types. A girl couldn't be too sure about the motives of the fast crowd. Even though things had sped up for Kelly, she wasn't ready to blast off into hyperspace just yet.

Of all the boys who had flirted with her during the first day of school, Kelly had been drawn to Brad Edwards, a shy, cute, intelligent senior who captained the swimming team and excelled in academics. Despite his gorgeous blue eyes, thick, sandy hair, and muscular build, Brad was not a typical athlete. He didn't seem to be stuck on himself like Jeremy and the other members of the football team. Brad was modest and hardworking. He had been nice to Kelly in chemistry class but he hadn't pushed her for a date, to her disappointment.

Kelly hoped that Brad would ask her out. She was pretty sure he would. And if he didn't, she was going to ask him. After all, it wasn't out of line for the girl to ask. Not if she really liked the boy.

"Kelly, can I come in?"

Her aunt was in the hall, tapping on her door.

"Sure, come on in, Aunt Doris."

Doris Hendricks cracked open the door and peeked into Kelly's bedroom. "Hi, honey. Would you like something to eat? I stopped on the way home and picked up burgers and fries."

Kelly shook her head. "No thanks. I'm not hungry."

Aunt Doris frowned. "Kelly, you have to eat. I mean, if you start skipping meals it could be dangerous. Have you ever heard of anorexia?"

Kelly shrugged. "I'm not anorexic, Aunt Doris. Don't worry, I'll fix a salad for myself later."

"Well, don't wait too long. It's almost six-thirty now."

"I'm fine, Aunt Doris, really."

Her aunt lingered in the doorway. "So, how was your first day back at school?"

"Great! I love all my classes. And I've made a lot of new friends."

"Oh. Well, I'm glad to hear that. Sometimes I wish I had more friends. It's not easy to make new friends when you get older."

Kelly picked up the mirror again, looking at her face. "Uh-huh."

"Are you sure you won't have something to eat?"

Kelly exhaled impatiently. "Aunt Doris, I told you, I don't want any of that greasy stuff you bring home. I don't want to get fat again."

A hurt expression came over her aunt's worn face. "Oh. Well, I'm sorry if I offended you, your highness. I didn't realize that I'm not good enough for you now that you've been promoted to princess." She started to leave in a huff.

Kelly jumped off the bed. "Aunt Doris, wait."

Her aunt turned back with a tear in her eye.

"I—I'm sorry," Kelly said. "I didn't mean to upset you. It's just . . . this is the first time I've been happy in a long time. I don't want to go back to being the way I was. Please, please try to understand that. I didn't mean to hurt your feelings."

Her aunt offered a weak smile. "It's all right. I do understand. It's just that I don't want to lose you, Kelly. You're the only relative I have left. Your mother's death hurt me too. When I look at you now, I see Lilah. You look just like her since you lost all that weight."

Kelly put her hand on her aunt's shoulder. "You won't lose me."

Doris Hendricks nodded. "I know. I just don't want all of this stuff to go to your head. You know how important it is for you to maintain your grades. I can't afford to send you to college, so a scholarship is your only chance. You've come too far to blow it now."

Kelly gave her aunt a little hug. "Don't worry, I won't blow it. I was just about to get started on my homework when you knocked. I'm not going to let you down. I promise."

"You've always been a good girl, Kelly. I want to give you your freedom, but I'd hate to see you change for the worse. I know I've been hard on you, but I've just tried to do what I thought your mother would want. I hope you—"

The phone rang in the hallway, interrupting the tender moment.

Kelly brushed past her aunt. "I'll get it." It might be Brad, calling to ask her out.

"Oh, hi, Rachel."

"Hi, Kelly," Rachel replied on the other end of the line. "I waited for you after school but you never showed up. I thought we were going to walk home together. I looked, but I couldn't find you."

"I'm sorry," Kelly said with a genuine tone of apology. "I was talking to Brad Edwards after chemistry class. I walked him over to the pool. Rachel, he's *sooo* sweet, you wouldn't believe it."

Rachel laughed and squealed with glee. "Brad Edwards! Forget about sweet. He's so cute!"

"You don't have to tell me!" Kelly replied.

"Are you going to go out with him?"

Kelly sighed. "I hope so. He didn't ask me. He's kind of shy. I like that. Not pushy like some other jerks."

A dreamy note came into Rachel's voice. "Oh,

that would be so cool if he asked you to the Back-to-School dance next Friday."

Kelly crossed her fingers. "I know it will happen."

"Hey," Rachel said, "you want to come over to study? You can tell me all about it."

Kelly considered for a minute. "Oh, I'd love to, but I can't. I have so much to do. I need to soak my contacts and get my clothes ready for tomorrow."

Rachel hesitated for a moment. "Oh, I see. Now that you're the most popular girl at Central—"

"No, no, it's not that," Kelly said. "Rachel! Why don't you come over here?"

Rachel sighed. "I'm sorry. I can't come over. I have to babysit my cousin. He's only three."

Kelly laughed. "Thank goodness, for a moment I thought you were mad at me. You aren't mad, are you?"

"No. I'm sorry again. I'll see you tomorrow."

"We'll walk to school," Kelly said. "See ya."

Kelly hung up and went back to her bedroom. She didn't think much about Rachel's sudden outburst. She had a lot to do if she was going to maintain her good looks.

When she had put her contacts into the soaking solution and laid out her clothes for the next day, Kelly sat on her bed again and picked up her chemistry book. For a moment, she found herself thinking about Brad. He was so handsome and sweet. She imagined what it would be like to kiss him.

"No," she said to herself. "I have to study. Aunt Doris is right about that scholarship."

But as soon as she opened the book, something fluttered out, landing on her bedspread. It was a piece of paper with something scrawled across it. Kelly's eyes focused on the one word message: "Fool!"

Kelly touched the weird-looking ink. Only it didn't appear to be ink at all, rather some kind of reddish-brown paint.

Dried blood?

Kelly wadded up the paper and flung it into her wastebasket. The bloody note was obviously some kind of prank played by Liza Brown or some other envious jerk. She wasn't going to let them spoil her fun. After all, popular kids often had to endure the slings and arrows of the less fortunate, those jealous people who didn't want anyone to have a good time.

Kelly would never again let them get to her.

They weren't going to take away her happiness.

Not in a million years.

She lowered her eyes to the page of the book and caught sight of the hand mirror in her peripheral vision. Putting the book down, she picked up the mirror. Kelly studied her smooth face, wondering if there were any other ways to make herself more beautiful.

EIGHT

After the final bell on Friday, Rachel and Marshall waited in front of Central, watching for Kelly. They needed to talk to Kelly about the election of new officers for the Computer Club. Marshall thought Kelly was a cinch to be chosen president now that she had become so popular. How could anyone oppose Central Academy's hottest rising star?

"Do you see her?" Marshall asked in a slightly hostile tone.

Rachel shook her head. "Not yet. She's been walking with Brad to the pool all week. It may be a few more minutes."

Marshall sighed and glared into the thinning crowd. "I wonder what she sees in that guy anyway?"

"Get real," Rachel replied. "He's cute *and* nice."

"I don't like him," Marshall muttered.

He would never have a chance with Kelly now. He had been looking forward to their senior year, sure that their love would blossom. Kelly had really let him down. He wasn't even sure he could be friends with her now.

Rachel fought the urge to feel resentful toward Kelly. After all, a best friend should be happy to see another friend's dreams coming true. Isn't that what every geeky kid wanted deep inside, the secret wish to become popular overnight? Kelly had done it in one week. Except for their morning walks to school, Kelly had been spending very little time with Rachel. Rachel refused to be bitter. It just wasn't in her nature to hold a grudge.

"There she is," Marshall said, pointing at Kelly.

Rachel bit her lip. Her heart had begun to pound. Something didn't feel right. What if Kelly didn't want to be friends with them anymore?"

"Maybe we shouldn't bother her," Rachel said.

Marshall grimaced, scowling at Kelly. "No, we'll give the little store-bought queen a chance. I mean, we have to ask her. She's still in the club."

I just hope she's still interested in the club, Rachel thought.

They moved on an intersecting path, catching Kelly at the steps. Rachel was nervous. It was almost like they were approaching a stranger, one of those popular kids who had never treated them decently in three years of high school.

"Hi," Kelly said. "I just walked Brad to the pool for swimming practice."

Marshall exhaled and stiffened. He felt horrible. He had lost Kelly to a likeable, good-looking guy. They'd never get together now. Never!

"He still hasn't asked me to the dance," Kelly said to Rachel. "But I know he's going to."

"Who cares?" Marshall snorted with venom on his lips. "We have to ask you something else. Are you going to run for president of the Computer Club?"

The question caught Kelly unaware. "Gee, I hadn't really thought about it. When are the elections?"

Marshall started to say something but Rachel elbowed him in the ribs. "Ow, why'd you do that?"

Rachel ignored him, smiling at Kelly. "We're the executive committee," she told Kelly. "We have to get together. How about tonight?"

Kelly shook her head. "I can't tonight. Brad and I are going to the football game."

"But you hate football," Marshall groaned.

Rachel hated football too, but she knew she would go to a game with a guy like Brad. She would go almost anywhere with him. As left out as Rachel was, she could not blame Kelly for choosing a cool boyfriend over the Computer Club.

Kelly frowned at her best friend. "Rachel, is everything all right?"

Marshall answered the question himself. "Nothing is all right, Kelly. You've changed. You're forgetting about your real friends, the people who have been loyal to you all these years."

"That's not fair!" Kelly snapped. "Just because I

didn't fall in love with you, Marshall, that doesn't mean—"

"Forget it!" Marshall cried. "I don't know why I even bothered."

Rachel tried to play mediator. "Come on Marshall, don't be this way."

Marshall shook his finger at Kelly. "From now on, you're out of the club. I'm throwing you out!"

"Fine by me," Kelly replied. "That's a club for geeks anyway."

Rachel felt a sudden sting in her heart. "Kelly, please—"

Marshall's face had turned slightly purple. He could not even speak now. He just turned and ran, almost stumbling on the concrete steps as he fled.

Kelly immediately regretted everything she had said. "Marshall!" she called after him.

Rachel put a hand on her forearm. "Don't worry, Kelly. He'll be all right. I think he just had to get it out of his system."

Kelly sighed. "Was I too tough on him?"

"Yes, but he was asking for it."

Kelly looked sideways at Rachel. "Do you think I've changed? Do you think I'm stuck up?"

Rachel lowered her head. "Well, you've changed, Kelly. But—"

Kelly's eyes grew wide. "Oh, so you think the same as Marshall?"

"No, that's not what I—"

Kelly brushed past Rachel, heading down the steps. "Forget it, Rachel. If you don't want to be friends with me, I can live with it. I have lots of friends now, friends who accept me the way I am."

"Kelly!"

"Good-bye, Rachel. You can walk to school with someone else on Monday."

"But I don't think you're stuck up!" Rachel cried.

But it was too late. Kelly did not seem to hear her. She just kept walking toward Rockbury Lane.

"Oh no," Rachel moaned.

She had just lost her best friend over a stupid misunderstanding. It was horrible. But not nearly as horrible as what was to come.

Kelly knew that she and Brad were building up to their first kiss. It had to happen. The evening had been too perfect for it *not* to happen.

He had picked her up, right on time, making small talk with Aunt Doris, who seemed to like him. Brad looked so wholesome in his white letter sweater and red swim-team shirt. Kelly also looked great in a pair of black jeans and a brown sweater. Aunt Doris said they were a handsome couple.

In the car, on the way to the stadium, Brad opened up a little, apologizing for the blue Honda Civic that was almost ten years old. Kelly didn't care about his car. She was happy just to be with him, even at a football game.

Kelly didn't pay much attention to Jeremy Rice's all-star performance as Central Academy walloped Elliot High, 47–10. She was too busy huddling with Brad, using every Central touchdown as an excuse to hug him. The expression on his sweet face told her that he really cared. Was he too shy to say it aloud?

After the game, they went for a drive along the coastal highway. Brad suggested a stop at Lighthouse Point. From there, they would be able to see the bright beam as it swept over the black ocean.

Kelly hesitated, but she finally agreed. She had to trust Brad sooner or later. Besides, she *wanted* him to kiss her. And she knew he was too much of a gentleman to try anything more than a kiss.

They parked in the empty lot below the point. The shoreline walk was open until midnight. Brad and Kelly climbed the concrete steps to the observation deck above them, over the rocks. They stood in the rotating beam of the lighthouse across the bay.

A brisk wind hit them in the face with salty sea air. Waves crashed on the dark shoreline. Kelly drew closer to Brad, wrapping her arms around his waist. He held her tightly in his strong arms.

Brad looked down into her face. "You want to walk on the beach?"

Kiss me, Kelly wished. Now!

"The water's a little rough—"

Suddenly the beam of the lighthouse swung around, flashing on them again. Kelly saw his handsome face in front of her. She could no longer hold back. Grabbing his face, she pressed her lips to his and kissed him until the light swung back around once more.

Kelly drew back, gasping for air. "Wow."

Brad lowered his head again. He kissed her firmly and started to pull her closer. Kelly kissed him back for a moment and then pushed him gently away from her.

"Kelly?"

She put her hand in the middle of his chest. "Slowly, Brad. You know I'm not the fast type."

He seemed disappointed but he nodded politely. "Sure, Kelly . . . it's just, that was great. One more kiss?"

She touched his face again. "Well, I guess one more wouldn't hurt."

They kissed as the waves crashed below them. When they broke apart, Kelly felt wild, adventurous. She wanted to walk on the beach, to feel the sea spray from the roaring surf.

Brad grabbed her hand. "Come on."

They descended to the beach on another set of concrete stairs. It was high tide, so one little strip of sand remained for their walk. The sea pounded the coast, churning the waters of the Atlantic. But it was somehow exciting to them, a tempestuous beginning to their romance.

"We have to go back," Brad said finally. "It's almost eleven-thirty."

"I don't care," Kelly replied.

"But your Aunt Doris—"

Kelly protested, but Brad prevailed, convincing her to do the responsible thing. If Aunt Doris got mad, she might not let them keep dating. Brad couldn't stand it if they couldn't see each other.

Kelly kissed him for that compliment. It was all

Brad could do to muster the strength to turn her toward the steps. If they hurried, they could make it home before midnight.

As they came to the bottom of the steps, Kelly gazed upward to the observation platform. At that moment, the beam from the lighthouse swung across the railing of the platform. Kelly startled and stepped back.

Brad lifted his eyes to the railing. "What is it?"

"I—I saw somebody," Kelly whispered. "In the light. There."

The light washed over the platform again. Kelly saw the human silhouette in the spectral ray. It seemed to be a man, standing at the top of the stairs. He was looking down at them.

"Did you see him?" Kelly asked.

Brad nodded. "I think I saw two of them."

Kelly's hand went to her throat. "Two of them?"

Suddenly the air felt chill and damp. She began to shiver. Then Brad broke away from her.

"Where are you going?" she cried above the surf.

Brad pointed upward. "Let me have a look. I'll come back for you."

"No!" She took a step after him. "Please, don't leave me here alone."

Brad kissed her cheek. "It'll be all right. I won't let anything happen to you. Just stay here for a minute."

Brad started toward the top of the platform, clutching the safety rail. Kelly wanted to follow him, but she could barely move. Suddenly her body had gone stiff in the wind. She wasn't dressed warmly enough for a September night at the beach.

"Brad!"

He could not hear her. She marked his progress with each swing of brilliance from the lighthouse. Brad was taking his time, creeping toward the platform in a slow, deliberate manner.

Kelly focused her eyes beyond his climbing figure. The lighthouse bathed the platform in the white glow. Kelly was certain that she saw a human being perched at the rail. They never should have come down to the beach.

"Brad!"

He reached the top step, disappearing onto the platform. Kelly kept her eyes trained on the railing. When the light swept over the platform, she could no longer see Brad. He was gone!

She couldn't wait for him to come back. Something awful had happened. She just knew it. He was up there, badly in need of her help.

Clinging to the safety rail, Kelly took each slippery step with caution. There was no other route to the highway unless she wanted to scale the rocks that formed the bulkhead above the beach. She had to cross the platform to get back to the other steps that led down to the parking lot.

As she neared the top of the landing, Kelly flashed on the nightmare she experienced before her sixteenth birthday. When she came up onto the platform, she peered toward the other set of stairs. The lighthouse beam swept over her shoulder. There was no one to block her path. The observation platform was empty.

What if the dark figures had simply been tricks of the light?

"Brad?"

She took a step toward the opposite side of the platform. Maybe Brad had gone to check on the car. Would he really leave her alone this long?

Kelly had almost reached the stairs when the light suddenly illuminated a man's shape in front of her. Kelly froze in the stiff breeze. The man started to move toward her.

"Brad!"

She backpedaled, slipped on the slick surface of the platform, and stumbled against the rail. The man lunged for her. She felt herself going over the side. Kelly managed to grab the wet railing that barely gave her purchase.

A hand closed on her wrist. If Kelly let go, she would tumble into the rocks below. Even if the fall did not kill her, she would surely break an arm or a leg. But if she hit her head . . .

"Kelly, it's me!"

The man's other hand gripped her forearm.

"Kelly, let me pull you up!"

Her eyes lifted to see Brad's face glowing in the lighthouse beam. "Brad! Help me! Please!"

Brad struggled to keep his grip on her. He managed to pull her over the rail. Kelly rolled, hitting the platform with a dull thud. Brad swept her up and wrapped her in his arms.

"What were you thinking?" Brad asked.

Tears flowed from her blurry eyes. "I—I thought you were hurt. I . . . oh, Brad, where did you go?"

Brad stroked her wet hair. "I thought I saw someone around the car. I went to look. I figured you'd be safer here."

Kelly sat up straight. "You saw someone?"

Brad nodded. "I think there was another car. I just saw a flash of red when I—"

"Jeremy!" Kelly cried. "It has to be him. He had a red car."

Brad grimaced. "I just saw a flash of red. It could have been a taillight as they turned onto the road."

Kelly shivered. "Let's get out of here."

"I'm for that," Brad replied.

They worked their way slowly back to the car where they found a nasty surprise. One of Brad's tires had been slashed.

"Jeremy," Kelly said again. "Doesn't he have anything better to do than torture me?"

Brad went for the trunk and the spare tire. "Now, Kelly, you don't know that for a fact. If you—" He stopped in midsentence, staring at the word that had been spray painted in red across the back windshield.

Kelly grew angry when she saw the same word that had appeared on the note in her textbook: *Fool!*

"Jeremy," Kelly muttered. "I bet Liza put him up to it."

"Why them?"

Kelly sighed. "They both have it in for me."

Brad shook his head. "I hate this kind of childish bull—"

"I know," Kelly replied. "So do I."

Brad began to change the tire. "I'm going to have a talk with Jeremy."

"No, please don't," Kelly said. "I mean, I'd like to get even with him as much as you, but leave it alone."

Brad stood up, wiping the sweat from his forehead. "Hey, I know how to fight. I don't like to do it, but sometimes you have to call out a bully like Rice. It's the only way."

Kelly was surprised, afraid, and delighted to see this new side of Brad. She put her hands on his shoulders. Before he could say another word, she kissed him again.

Brad was the one who drew back this time. "Kelly . . ."

She frowned, expecting the worst. "What?"

He sighed. "Would you go to the dance with me next Friday?"

"Of course."

"And . . ." He hesitated, taking a deep breath. "Will you wear my ring?"

Kelly forgot about everything else that had happened that night. He was asking her to go steady! She hadn't been expecting this, especially not on their first date.

"I like you a lot," Brad went on. "I'm afraid some other guy is going to get you. I—"

She pressed her fingertips to his mouth. "Don't

say another word. Yes, I'll go to the dance. And I'll think about going steady. Okay?"

"When will you tell me?"

She smiled. "Friday at the dance." That would give it some suspense, though she was fairly certain that she would accept his class ring.

"How about another kiss?" Brad asked with a smile.

Kelly pointed to the car. "How about changing that tire first?"

Brad pretended to pout. "Am I finished with kisses for the evening?"

Kelly winked at him. "Oh, I think you've got a chance at the door, you know. A good-night kiss."

"Don't you mean a sympathy kiss?"

Kelly pushed him away from her. "Change the tire." She grinned.

Even with the setback of the slashed tire, Brad had her back at MacDonald Avenue five minutes before midnight. Aunt Doris had left on the porch light. Kelly gave Brad a good-night kiss and hurried up the stone walkway. She was grinning as she entered the townhouse.

"Aunt Doris?"

There was no reply.

Maybe her aunt had fallen asleep already. Kelly didn't have anything to worry about. The clock was just striking midnight as she started for the stairs.

Kelly startled when the phone rang in the hall.

Who would be calling this late? She grabbed the receiver on the second ring, praying that the clamor had not awakened her aunt.

"Hello?"

There was a pause on the other end of the line. Kelly could hear someone breathing. She was about to hang up when a weird voice crackled out of the earpiece. Kelly didn't hear it clearly at first. But some strange compulsion caused her to lift the receiver to her ear.

"Hello?" she said again.

"You little fool."

It was obviously someone trying to disguise his or her voice.

"Is that you, Jeremy?" Kelly warned. "I'm going to call the police if you don't stop this."

"This isn't Jeremy."

"Very funny," Kelly replied. "I know it's you, Jeremy. Brad didn't appreciate you slashing his tire."

"Fool!"

"Is that the only word you know?" Kelly challenged. "This is junior high stuff, Jeremy. I'm going to hang up."

"Sweet sixteen," the voice said.

"Get lost, Jeremy. Or is this Liza?"

"This isn't Liza."

"Who is it then?" Kelly demanded.

"Sweet sixteen, you'll never see seventeen!"

Kelly flashed back to the dream, when another eerie voice had said the same thing. No one could know about the nightmare. Kelly hadn't told anyone, not even Rachel. It had to be a coincidence.

"Drop dead," Kelly told the voice.

She slammed down the phone and unplugged it from the wall. That would keep Jeremy and Liza quiet for the night. How could they be such jerks? If only there was some way to fix them forever!

Kelly was halfway up the stairs when she saw her aunt standing at the top of the landing, clad in her gray housecoat.

"I heard voices," Aunt Doris said sleepily. "And the phone was ringing."

"Just a prank call," Kelly replied.

Aunt Doris squinted at her. "You look scared."

Kelly shook her head, realizing that her hands were trembling a little. "I'm okay. I just got home. I was in before twelve."

"Suit yourself. I'm going back to bed."

Kelly ran into her room, closing and locking the door. She was scared and happy at the same time. Everything was moving too fast. What if it got out of hand?

She wouldn't give up her relationship with Brad, not for anything. They'd just have to weather the storm. Jeremy and Liza had to ease off sooner or later. Kelly could wait them out. Her love was strong enough to endure any obstacle.

By the time she was ready for bed, rain had begun to pelt her bedroom window. The wind blew strong over Port City, bringing a gale from the east. Kelly slid under her comforter, listening to the rain. It took her a long time to fall asleep. When sleep finally came, she dreamed of storm-tossed waters, evil phone calls, and the kisses of the sweetest boy she had ever known.

NINE

Kelly didn't see Brad again over the weekend but she talked to him on Saturday and Sunday. They spent hours on the phone, chatting until Aunt Doris picked up the downstairs extension and told Kelly to cut it short. Kelly almost died of embarrassment, although Brad seemed to understand. He was the greatest. Kelly was tempted to accept his class ring and go steady with him right then and there. But she finally decided to play it out, to enjoy every moment of their developing affection.

Brad agreed to meet Kelly at the Central campus early Monday morning. She couldn't wait to see him. She left for school wearing a blue denim jacket, a white turtleneck, and stone-washed jeans. The weather was growing cool enough for her to wear some of the new things she had purchased for fall.

Kelly kept her eyes straight forward as she passed Rachel's house. They hadn't spoken since their fight on Friday. Kelly felt badly that they weren't talking, but she wasn't ready to give in and make friends again. Rachel was just jealous, like Marshall. They had no right to judge Kelly just because she had achieved the status that everyone else wanted. How could they be mad about her newfound success?

When she reached the park, Kelly relaxed. It did seem a little lonely to walk to school by herself. But she would soon see Brad. Her Brad. Her first boyfriend! Nothing could spoil that happiness.

In her mind, she could hear Rachel saying, "Don't be stupid! Take the ring before he changes his mind!"

No! She had promised to give him an answer at the dance on Friday night. She would stick to that promise.

She came out of the park, crossing over Middle Road to Rockbury Lane. She hoped Brad was already there, waiting for her. If he came extra early, that meant he was anxious to see her. They would become Central's most popular couple in no time, replacing Jeremy and Liza, the duo from the dark side.

Kelly's pace quickened on Rockbury. She was almost on the school grounds when she glanced up to see Brad standing in the middle of the road. Only he was not looking in her direction. Instead, he was squaring off with Jeremy, toe-to-toe, nose-to-nose. Their faces were red with anger.

"Fight!" someone cried.

"No," Kelly muttered. "Not today."

She ran toward Brad, but it was too late. Kelly could not stop them. They were ready to fight.

Jeremy threw the first blow, a roundhouse right hand that appeared to graze Brad's face. Brad stumbled backward a few steps. Jeremy sprang after him, fists flying. Brad was going to get killed.

"Stop it!" Kelly shouted. "Stop it now!"

Kelly heard Liza's haughty laughter from the front seat of the red Buick Riviera that was parked at the curb. A crowd had started to gather to watch the combatants. Most of them seemed to be rooting for Jeremy, who apparently had landed several hard punches.

But Brad was not finished yet.

Jeremy had grown overconfident in his haste to beat down Brad. He swung wildly, arms flailing, leaving himself open. Suddenly Brad's foot flashed through the air in a low kick. Jeremy screeched and doubled over, grabbing his torso. Brad's kick had crunched Jeremy's ribs. The cracking sound made a few of the spectators groan in sympathetic agony.

Jeremy stayed down on one knee, gasping for air. "You broke my ribs," he whined. "Oww—"

"Get up," Brad challenged. "Come on, let's finish it now. You aren't so tough when somebody fights back."

But Jeremy was in no shape to continue. "Ow, it hurts," he moaned.

Liza jumped out of the red Buick, rushing to Jeremy's side. "What did you do to him, Brad?"

"I fought back," Brad replied. "Bullies aren't used to people fighting back. Are they, Jeremy?"

Kelly shoved her way through the ring of on-lookers to stand next to Brad. She put her hand on his shoulder. "Are you all right?"

Brad nodded, looking no worse for the violence. "I'm fine."

"Did you really have to fight him?"

"I'm sorry," Brad replied. "But he was asking for it."

Liza glared at Brad. "You didn't have to hurt him, Edwards!"

Kelly glared back, defending her champion. "Oh, shut up, Liza. We know you slashed our tire at Lighthouse Point."

"You're in big trouble," Jeremy moaned. "If this keeps me out of the game on Saturday—"

"No way. You're not gonna blame this on me." Brad insisted. "Ask anyone here. They'll tell you who really started this."

"Yeah," someone intoned from the crowd, "Jeremy was the one who started it. It's his own fault."

"It was Rice all the way."

"Jeremy threw the first punch."

The sentiments of the spectators had switched to the victor.

Suddenly the crowd parted to allow a tall, red-haired man to push his way to the source of the commotion. Assistant Principal Harlan Kinsley towered over Jeremy, who was still down. Kinsley's head turned, his keen eyes glaring at them one at a time. He demanded to know what had happened.

They were all silent, refusing to tell him. Nobody wanted to squeal on a classmate.

"You'd better come clean," Kinsley insisted. "If you don't, all of you will be suspended, effective right now!"

Still no reply from the hesitant students.

"I can't take a suspension," Brad whispered to Kelly. "The coach will throw me off the swimming team."

Kinsley put his hands on his hips. "I mean it. Tell me what happened or I'll take your names and—"

"Ask Jeremy," Kelly said. "He'll tell you."

Liza scowled at Kelly. "You little—"

Kinsley looked down at the boy who was on one knee. "What's the story, Rice? What happened here?"

Jeremy glanced up, gasping as he spoke. "Uh, I fell—"

"Fell?" Kinsley said in a disbelieving tone. "There are too many people here just to watch you fall."

"He did fall," Liza said. "It was an accident."

Kinsley squinted skeptically at them. "Are you sure? It looks more like a fight to me."

Jeremy stood slowly, holding his ribs. "No, I swear, I slipped and hit the curb. Brad was just trying to help me up."

He didn't want to get in trouble, Kelly thought.

Not with so many witnesses to say he started the fight.

Kinsley sighed, knowing that they were lying but unable to prove it. "Okay, let's break it up. Everyone scatter."

The students lingered for a moment to watch Jeremy, wondering if Brad had done some real damage. Most of the unpopular kids had suffered embarrassment or pain at the hands of Jeremy and Liza at some time. They were glad to see him get his comeuppance from a nice guy like Brad.

"I mean it!" Kinsley bellowed. "Get moving now. And Rice, you'd better come with me. Have the nurse take a look at those ribs."

"Yes sir."

Jeremy leaned on Liza as they started to follow Mr. Kinsley. Liza's narrow eyes shot daggers at Kelly. Kelly just ignored her. Maybe now Jeremy would leave them alone.

As the crowd began to disperse, Kelly hooked her arm through Brad's. "Are you all right?"

He nodded. "Yeah, he never really hit me."

"You were great," Kelly said. "Just great."

Brad sighed. "I don't use my self-defense training very often, but he had it coming."

Kelly frowned. "How did it start?"

"I don't know," Brad replied. "I walked over here to wait for you. I know you always walk down Rockbury."

Kelly felt warm inside. Brad *had* been anxious to see her. Their love was as strong as she had hoped it to be.

"Rice was in the car with Liza," Brad went on. "I tried to ignore them, but Jeremy wasn't ready to leave it alone. He said something hateful about you, Kelly."

"Me? What did that idiot say?"

Brad blushed and lowered his eyes. "I don't want to—"

"Go on, tell me!"

Brad exhaled. "He asked me what it was like to go out with a fat girl."

Kelly's eyes narrowed. "That rodent."

"Then I asked him if he had a good time slashing my tires at Lighthouse Point. Naturally, he denied it. Then he made another remark—"

"About me?"

"I'm not going to tell you what he said," Brad insisted. "It's too disgusting."

"I can imagine," Kelly said.

Brad shook his head. "I was ready to walk away when Liza jumped into it. She said something nasty and I told her to take off. That was when Jeremy decided that he wanted to fight."

Kelly wrapped her arms about his waist, hugging him, telling herself that everything was going to be all right. "I guess some jerks never know when to quit."

"Don't worry, it's over."

For now, Kelly thought. But she knew enough about Jeremy and Liza to figure that they wouldn't quit, especially now that Brad had gotten the better of them. It was only a matter of time before something else happened.

The first bell rang, echoing over the schoolyard.

"Come on," Brad said, "let's just forget about this."

Kelly gazed up into his soft eyes. "Would a kiss help?"

Brad smiled. "Now you're talking."

Their lips met in an innocent kiss that made Kelly feel better. After all, young lovers often had obstacles to overcome. They were like Romeo and Juliet—nothing could stand in their way.

Brad wanted a second kiss, but Kelly broke away.

"We're going to be late," she said.

Brad shrugged. "So what?"

"Oh, you!"

He walked her to homeroom, squeezing her hand before he disappeared into the classroom down the hall. They'd meet for lunch and she would see him in their last period class. Kelly thought she might even accompany him to the swimming pool and watch him practice. She wanted to spend every minute with him, and she was sure he felt the same way about her.

Homeroom was abuzz with rumors about the big fight. Everyone asked Kelly what had happened, but she kept quiet as she eased into her desk. She knew Brad was right; it was better to forget the whole thing. Only some people would not let it die.

A crackling noise came over the loudspeaker on the wall. Kelly leaned back in her desk, expecting the morning announcements. Instead, she got an unwelcome surprise.

"Kelly Langdon, please report to Miss Monica's office immediately. Kelly Langdon, please report—"

They all whispered and pointed as Kelly got out of her desk. She made her way through the empty hall, toward the administrative offices. Miss Monica was waiting behind her desk.

Kelly dropped into the wooden chair, shifting nervously. "Hi."

Miss Monica regarded her with an unreadable look. "Kelly, first off, let me say how proud I am of you. I gave you a chance and you didn't let me down. You've made quite a transformation since last year. You've turned into a lovely young lady."

Kelly blushed. "I appreciate what you did for me, Miss Monica. Did you get my thank-you card?"

Miss Monica nodded. "That was very thoughtful. But let's get to the point, Kelly. What happened this morning between Brad Edwards and Jeremy Rice?"

Kelly shrugged and hung her head. "Jeremy slipped and fell, that's all."

Miss Monica leaned forward on her desk. "Kelly, this is between you and me. Anything you say will stay in this office."

But Kelly shook her head, unrelenting. She could not betray Brad. If she told the truth, Brad could be in big trouble. She had to protect him.

Miss Monica sighed and leaned back in the chair. "Okay, you can go."

Kelly glanced up. "Really?"

"Yes. But keep this in mind, Kelly: I'm on your side. If you need any help, you can trust me. I don't like bullies. If Jeremy is causing problems for you, maybe I can help put an end to it."

"I'm fine, Miss Monica. Thanks for everything."

Kelly left the office in a hurry. She ran straight into Jeremy and Liza, who were sitting outside the nurse's office. Liza sneered and muttered something trashy as Kelly passed. Jeremy grimaced at her, still in pain.

What jerks! Kelly thought.

If only there was some way to get even with them, to fix them so they would leave her alone forever.

No! She wouldn't entertain notions of vengeance. That would only drag her down to their level.

She wouldn't hatch plots in her head or attack them. Not right away.

She'd wait until the dance on Friday.

TEN

Hundreds of stockinged feet shuffled on the wooden floor of the Central Academy gymnasium, bodies writhing in time to the thump of an electric bass guitar. The Back-to-School dance was a wild sock hop, fueled by the hard rock sound of a group called Steelhead. Everyone had removed their shoes at the door because the coaches didn't want anyone scuffing the basketball court. Kelly was having a great time.

Kelly had never been to a dance before so she worried that she might make a fool of herself on the gym floor. At first, she found it awkward to slide across the polished surface in her socks. Brad had to catch her a couple of times to keep her from falling.

Brad had been wonderful and understanding, his usual self. He told her to slow down, to watch the other kids. Just do what they do and invent a few personal moves. The important thing was to listen to the beat.

Kelly immediately keyed in on the bass guitar, surrendering to the primal rhythm and following Brad, who was a solid dancer. By the end of the first set, Kelly had improved dramatically. Of course, the slow dances came easy since she got to put her arms around Brad and draw close to him. She felt safe and secure with him holding her.

At the end of the second set, Kelly was ready to take a break. Brad held her hand, leading her to the refreshment table where Rachel and Marshall were serving as concessionaires. They earned extra money for the Computer Club treasury by working at the dance.

As soon as Kelly saw Rachel, she regretted the misunderstanding that had driven them apart. Was it too late to put things right? Kelly tried to make eye contact, but Rachel ignored her as she filled the punch bowl.

Marshall was a little more obvious. He glared at Brad like he wanted to start an argument, but Brad didn't seem to notice. He just filled two cups with punch and handed one of them to Kelly.

"Thanks," Kelly said glumly, looking away from her former friends.

Brad squinted at her. "Is everything all right?"

Kelly sighed. She had to talk to Rachel. She didn't want their friendship to end over something silly. They had been best friends since junior high.

Kelly gazed into Brad's concerned eyes. "Uh, could I have a minute alone with Rachel?"

Brad shrugged. "Sure. Hey, the band's on a break. I'm going to go backstage and talk to my friend Paul. He's the drummer." He gave her a kiss on the cheek and walked away.

Kelly turned quickly to Rachel. "Can't we just talk this out?"

Rachel looked back at her, not saying a word.

Marshall, however, was in full voice. "Well, if it isn't Miss Central, Kelly, Queen of the Universe. She deigns to talk to us."

Kelly grimaced. "It's not like that, Marshall."

"We don't need your pity or your charity," Marshall went on, his face red. "You're popular now, too good to hang with your old friends. You—"

"Oh, shut up, Marshall!"

Rachel had bellowed the command, not Kelly.

Marshall wheeled to gaze wild-eyed at Rachel. "Don't tell me you're on her side. Traitor!"

Rachel pushed him toward the other end of the table. "We're out of cookies. Get some more."

Marshall hesitated, his angry eyes flashing at Kelly. He had loved her so much for so long. He had loved her when she was still a fat nerd. Why couldn't she be *his* girl? Clenching his fists in the air, he turned away from them, muttering to himself.

"Sorry," Rachel said. "Marshall has a big mouth."

Kelly shook her head. "No, I'm the one who should be sorry. I went off on you the other day. I apologize."

Rachel looked at the punch bowl. "It's all right. You and Brad look *tres* happy."

"Thanks, we are. He asked me to go steady."

An expression of glee spread over Rachel's face. "No way! What did you tell him?"

"I'm supposed to give him my answer tonight."

Rachel leaned on the table, gawking at her. "Are you crazy? Get the class ring now, before he changes his mind."

Kelly started to laugh. Rachel made a face and broke into a chuckle. They were friends again, and it felt like a weight had been lifted from their souls.

Kelly grinned broadly. "Call you tomorrow?"

"Sure."

"Tell Marshall I—"

Rachel waved her off. "Don't worry about him. He won't go ballistic again. I'll have a talk with him."

"Do you think I've been too hard on him?" Kelly asked.

"He's just jealous. Don't worry about it. Go have a good time. If I was with a guy like Brad, I wouldn't be here behind this punch bowl."

"You're the greatest, Rachel. See you tomorrow."

Kelly was elated as she went off to look for Brad. She had her best friend again. She had missed Rachel terribly, more than she had realized. It would be great to share everything new and exciting, although Kelly knew she had to tone it down a bit so Rachel wouldn't be envious.

Brad was nowhere to be found. The stage was empty, so he had to be in the backstage area

talking to his friend. Kelly found a side door that
led into the wings. When Mr. Kinsley wasn't
looking, she ducked through the entrance to find
herself in a long, shadowy corridor.

Muffled voices echoed through the darkness.
She felt her way along the brick wall, hesitating
when she thought she heard Brad's familiar tone.
Was she getting closer to him?

"Brad? Brad, are you there?"

The voices faded. Had they heard her? Kelly
started to move forward. She heard only silence.

"Brad?"

Another set of footsteps reverberated in the corridor. Someone was walking behind her. She took a
deep breath, turning toward the male figure.

"Brad?"

"Yeah, babe?"

She took a step toward him in the dim light.
"Brad, thank goodness you—"

But it wasn't Brad.

Suddenly the looming shape sprang at her,
leaping like a predatory animal. Kelly felt his
hands on her shoulders. He pushed her back
against the brick wall. His face bent toward her,
easy to recognize in the dim light.

"You!" Kelly said.

Jeremy Rice grinned at her, keeping her pinned
with his superior weight. "What're you doing back
here, sweetie?"

Kelly squirmed against the wall. "Let me go, or
I'll scream!"

"Take it easy—"

"I mean it," Kelly insisted. "Brad is back there. You want a repeat performance?"

Jeremy eased back a little. "He didn't hurt me. I'm playing in the game tomorrow. It was just a bruise."

"Too bad," Kelly said.

She tried to move around him.

Jeremy stopped her again. "Hey, I thought you and me could head over to the pool. Maybe take a little dip. A skinny dip!"

Kelly smiled. Her fears vanished, giving way to a strange notion that had begin to hatch in her mind. She had taken enough grief from Jeremy. Now it was time for some solid payback. It was going to be a harmless but humiliating prank.

She feigned interest in his offer, looking up innocently. "You mean, you can get into the pool this time of night?"

Jeremy bristled, puffing out his chest like a vain rooster. "Hey, I can get in any time."

"What about Liza?" Kelly asked.

Jeremy shrugged. "Forget about her. We're through. I really like you, Kelly. I want you a lot more than I want Liza."

"The pool, huh? And a skinny dip?"

Jeremy pressed against her. "Don't tell me you're interested?"

Kelly smiled. "Maybe. That is, *if* you can break into the pool dome."

He grabbed her hand. "Come on, I'll show you."

Kelly's pulse was throbbing in her temples as Jeremy led her through the shadows. What if

Brad saw them? They left the gym through a back door, emerging into the cool night. Kelly had dressed for fall in her denim outfit complete with a black turtleneck sweater. The ground was still cold on her stockinged feet.

Jeremy was also shoeless. He wore a punky, loose-fitting jacket of brown linen that was cut in a double-breasted style. He did make quite a handsome figure in his expensive button-down shirt and khaki chinos. That fact only sweetened what she had planned for him.

They approached the swimming dome, which was dark inside. Jeremy led her to a side door where they stopped. Kelly glanced around, hoping that no one had seen them leave together. She didn't want Brad to find out what she was doing, at least until after it had happened. This was between her and Jeremy.

"Are you sure you can get us in?" Kelly asked.

Jeremy gave a cocky laugh. "In my sleep. Wait here."

He disappeared, leaving Kelly alone in the shadows. What if this was another one of Jeremy's hateful tricks? She heard the door rattling in front of her. It swung open. Jeremy filled the doorway.

"We're in," he said. "Hurry, before someone sees us."

Kelly followed him into the stillness of the pool dome. The only light was the one at the deep end of the Olympic-sized pool. Jeremy led her to the edge of the water.

"Lets get naked," he said, starting to take off his coat.

Kelly grimaced. "I don't know. That water looks pretty cold. We'll freeze."

"Naw, it's heated," Jeremy said, throwing his coat onto the floor.

Kelly kept up the pretense. "Well, maybe if I could feel the water first."

Jeremy gestured to the eerie green glow of the pool. "Be my guest."

She inched next to him, putting her hand on his shoulder. "Uh, I can't bend over in these tight jeans. I was wondering if you could, oh, I don't know, maybe put some of the pool water on your lips. Then I could kiss you and I'd be able to see how hot it is. Or how hot *you* are."

Jeremy smiled. It was working.

"I knew you'd be a little kinky," he told her, bending in with his mouth half open.

Kelly put her fingertips on his chin, stopping him. "Wet them first. And then we'll . . . Oh, I can't bring myself to say it."

Jeremy gave a sweeping bow. "Your wish is my pleasure, babe. One set of wet lips, coming up."

He took the bait like a hungry carp. Jeremy knelt at the edge of the pool. He reached out his hand to scoop up some of the heated water. His back was exposed to Kelly, an unsuspecting, vulnerable posture.

"Wet this!" Kelly cried, as she put her foot in the middle of his back. One healthy shove sent Jeremy plummeting into the pool, fully clothed. He came up treading water. Kelly picked up his coat and swung it over her head.

"Not the coat!" Jeremy cried.

She threw it into the pool with him. Jeremy screeched, grabbing the fancy garment as it soaked. He swam into the shallow end and stood up near the concrete steps in the corner.

"You witch!" he cried.

Kelly scowled at him. "That's what you get for bothering me."

"Enough already!" Jeremy cried. "How much do I have to suffer for a few wisecracks and that pizza thing?"

"What about the prank phone calls?" Kelly challenged. "And that bloody note?"

"I don't know what you're talking about! I swear."

"What about slashing our tire at Lighthouse Point?"

He played the baffled innocent. "I don't know anything about that. I never slashed anything!"

"Liar!"

"Kelly, listen to me, please—"

She pointed at him. "You listen to me, Jeremy. I've had it with your games. You stay away from me and Brad and leave us alone."

"I never—"

"Or I'll tell Mr. Kinsley all about your little game."

"Kelly—"

"Miss Monica is on to you," Kelly said. "She'll back me up if I want to bring charges. Do you understand?"

Jeremy threw up his dripping hands. "I never did—"

"*Do you understand?*"

He nodded. "Okay, okay. I'm finished with you, you nutso babe. But you better stay away from me too."

"I don't think that will be a problem."

Kelly wheeled on the balls of her feet and stomped toward the exit door. She left the pool dome, hurrying back to the gymnasium. The back door was locked, so she had to enter through the front. It took her a while to find Brad. He didn't even ask her where she had been.

Kelly breathed easier, knowing that she had left Jeremy standing knee-deep in the water. He hadn't been expecting his "romantic" encounter to backfire. She had put out his flames in a hurry.

She began to dance again with Brad. He asked her why she looked so happy. She told him that she was just happy to be with him.

Kelly drew closer to him, putting her head on his shoulder during a slow number. As they twirled in perfect harmony, Kelly heard Liza's voice rising above the music. Liza's blond head bobbed between the dancers. Her mouth was flapping as well.

"Have you seen Jeremy?" she kept asking.

Finally Liza came face to face with Brad and Kelly. She didn't ask *them* about her boyfriend. Liza turned away, looking in a different direction.

Kelly sighed contentedly, resting against Brad's firm body, wishing only that she could see Liza's face when she discovered her waterlogged boy-friend.

After Kelly left the pool area, Jeremy Rice surveyed his sorry state. He was wet and soggy. But he still had to laugh as he stood in the shallow end of the pool. Kelly had really gotten him good. Now he wanted her more than ever.

He waded to the concrete steps, dragging his coat behind him. The coat was ruined. His mother had paid more than a hundred dollars for the jacket. It had taken him all summer to talk her into buying it.

Jeremy sat on the edge of the pool, still dangling his feet in the water. He always got whatever he wanted in life—except for Kelly. He could not believe how much she had changed. How could a dumpy girl with glasses turn into a fox in a few short months? A real heartbreaker!

"Maybe she's got a deal with the devil," he said to himself.

He wasn't going to give up, not even with those bogus threats hanging over his head. Why had she gone on about phone calls and bloody notes? He had never done any of those things to her.

Maybe Liza had been working overtime. Liza could be a real terror. Jeremy didn't care about her. He sure didn't feel what he felt for Kelly. He just hung out with Liza because she knew how to show a boy a very good time.

Jeremy sighed in disgust. He knew he had to get to his car. If he went home and changed, he could come back to the dance without anyone else knowing what had happened.

Of course, he would have to come up with another way to get to Kelly. He wasn't going to leave it alone. He *had* to have her.

His head turned when he heard the back door open and close.

He smiled. "Well, you came back. Good, we can swim while my clothes dry out. If you're lucky, I'll show you a few new strokes."

He wasn't watching as the figure crept up behind him, lurking a few steps away. A pair of white hands clutched the handle of a small sledgehammer.

"Jeremy, look at me."

"Sure, babe, I—huh!?"

He was gaping over his shoulder when the hammer struck him solidly in the temple. The blow sent him hurtling into the pool with a splash. Blood began to seep from the gash in his head. His body rolled over in the water and floated face down as a stream of red slowly turned the blue water black.

ELEVEN

The incandescent ceiling lights burned low in the gymnasium, providing a romantic atmosphere for Kelly and Brad. They circled slowly on the dance floor, their bodies moving as one despite the fact that the band was playing a fast number. Brad looked into Kelly's eyes. She kissed him lightly on the lips. They felt like they were the only couple in the gym, in the world.

She put her lips close to his ear. "I love you," she whispered.

Brad drew back a little. "I love you too, but—"

Kelly's smooth face grew tense. "But what?" She hoped that he wasn't going to drop a bomb on her, not this late in the festivities.

His expression was dire, almost desperate. "You never gave me an answer to my question."

She decided to tease him a little. "Oh? What question was that?"

Brad grimaced. "Kelly! Be serious. I asked you

to go steady. You said you'd give me an answer tonight."

"I know."

He put his hands on his hips. "So?"

Kelly could never refuse him. There was no doubt in her mind. They were meant to be. The perfect couple.

Kelly winked at him. "Keep dancing. Come on, put your arms around me. I want you to hold me."

Brad embraced her again. "Kelly, I've never felt this way about anyone before. I don't want to lose you."

"You won't lose me, Brad."

He searched her hazel eyes hopefully. "Do you mean . . . ?"

Kelly wanted to hear herself saying the words, "Yes, Brad, I'll go steady with you."

But she never got the chance. Before her lips could move, a shrill cry pierced the thick air of the gymnasium. Even the band stopped playing. A girl was screaming at the top of her voice. Everyone turned to see who was disrupting the party.

"Help me! Please, help me!"

Brad stood on tiptoe, trying to see over the crowd. The dancers parted as the distraught girl pushed across the gym floor. Brad saw the thick mane of blond hair.

"Who is it?" Kelly asked.

"Liza," Brad replied. "And I think she's totally lost it."

Liza Brown burst through the crowd, stopping in front of Brad and Kelly. Black streaks of mascara flowed in the tears that striped her puffy face. Liza's whole body trembled as she tried to speak.

"Help me," she repeated. "Help him!" She pointed in the direction of the pool dome.

Kelly went limp. Liza was overreacting to Jeremy's untimely dip in the water. This had to be some kind of act, another trick to get even with Kelly.

Mr. Kinsley broke through the ring of onlookers who had surrounded them. "What's going on here?"

Liza grabbed his hands. "J-Jeremy," she stammered. "Jeremy is dead!"

A dull murmur rose in the gym as the students passed the news to the back of the crowd.

Mr. Kinsley held up his hands. "Everyone stay calm until we find out what happened. And nobody leave the gym."

He led Liza toward one of the back exits in the building.

Kelly's face had gone pale. Jeremy couldn't be dead. She had left him standing knee-deep in water. He had been alive and kicking. How could he be dead?

It was another trick. They were paying her back for pushing Jeremy in the pool. But why would they resort to something as dangerous as faking a death? A queasy sensation in her stomach warned Kelly that this might not be a ploy.

"Are you all right?" Brad asked.

She nodded absently. "Yeah, I'm okay."

Brad whistled and shook his head. "Man, did you see her face? I've never seen Liza that far gone."

She may take me with her, Kelly thought.

A paralyzing fear assaulted Kelly's body. What if she had caused Jeremy's death? What if he had slipped in the pool and knocked himself back into the water to drown? Wasn't that technically her fault since she had pushed him in the first place? The sound of police sirens drawing closer added to their curiosity—and Kelly's apprehension. The wait was killing her.

A few minutes later, Mr. Kinsley bolted onto the stage, and seized the microphone. "May I have your attention please? Will Kelly Langdon and Brad Edwards please report to the pool dome. That's Kelly Langdon and Brad Edwards. The rest of you are to go home now."

Brad looked at Kelly with a puzzled expression. "Us?"

Kelly could barely catch her breath but she managed to say, "Come on, let's find our shoes."

Police Chief Victor Danridge sat in a leather-covered chair, staring at the two upset teenagers on the other side of his desk. In his gray suit and shiny wing tips, Danridge looked the part of a career policeman: young, straightforward, and all business. He had not talked to Brad and Kelly at the poolhouse, the scene of the crime. His steely eyes flickered back and forth making them uneasy. Danridge finally began to address them in a friendly but distant manner.

"I asked you to come to the station because I wanted your parents to be here. Brad, your mother and father are outside in the waiting room. Kelly, I couldn't reach your aunt. Do you have any idea where she might be?"

Kelly shook her head. She could not shake the sight of Jeremy's body on a stretcher. His face had been covered with a white sheet. He really was dead. Liza wasn't playing one of her tricks this time.

"All right," Danridge said. "Let's get down to business. Brad, I understand you recently had a fight with Jeremy. Kicked him in the ribs."

Brad sat up straight, eager to tell the truth. "Yes, we had a fight. Jeremy started it. I just defended myself."

"Why didn't you tell Kinsley the truth when he broke up the fight?"

Brad sighed. "I didn't want to get Jeremy in trouble. He would've gotten kicked off the football team. I—I guess that doesn't matter now."

Danridge cast a searching look in Brad's direction. "Are you sure you weren't protecting yourself?"

"I told you, Jeremy started it. I wasn't going to let him punch me out. But I didn't want to hurt him."

Danridge turned to Kelly. "You had trouble with Jeremy too, didn't you?"

Kelly trembled, wondering how much she

should tell Danridge. Of course Jeremy had been horrible to her, but it wouldn't help her to go on about that now. It would only give her a motive for a terrible crime that she had not committed.

"Kelly?"

She had to say something. "He used to tease me," she replied quickly.

"Why?" Danridge asked.

"Because I wouldn't do his homework for him. And then—I think he has—*had*—a crush on me."

Brad touched Kelly's hand. "She's being easy on him, sir. Jeremy was rotten to both of us. He slashed my tire at Lighthouse Point. He sent nasty notes to Kelly and made crank phone calls."

"Is that true, Kelly?"

"Well, yes," she replied. "He bothered us, but Brad and I decided to ignore him. Then he picked a fight with Brad. I just wanted to forget about him."

Danridge leaned forward with his hands on the desktop. "Brad, would you mind giving me a moment alone with Kelly?"

"Sure." Brad squeezed her hand before he went into the outer office.

Kelly sat alone in the chair, her eyes trained on the floor. How long could she hide the simple truth that she had been the one who led Jeremy to the pool dome? What if someone had seen them together? The truth might ruin everything that she had worked so hard to achieve.

"Don't look so gloomy," Danridge said, trying to console her. "You aren't in any trouble, Kelly."

She glanced up, frowning at him. "I didn't hate Jeremy, not even for the things he did to me."

"You didn't want revenge?"

She shook her head. "No, I'm sorry he's dead. I'm really sorry."

"What about Brad? Did he want revenge?"

Her face went slack. "No. He's not like that."

Danridge made a note on a legal pad. "Kelly, were you with Brad tonight?"

She nodded weakly. "Yes."

"All night? The whole dance I mean?"

"Well, we were separated for a few minutes when he went backstage to see his friend in the band."

"And where were you during that time?"

Kelly's heart was searching for an escape route from her chest. "I—I was talking to my friend Rachel at the refreshment table."

"What's her last name?"

"Warren. Rachel Warren."

Danridge wrote it down and then leaned back in his chair, thinking. "How long were you and Brad separated?"

"Fifteen minutes."

"Hmm. Could it have been longer than fifteen minutes?"

"Maybe," Kelly replied.

"Longer than thirty minutes?"

"No."

"Kelly, did you actually see Brad with his friend in the band?"

She lowered her eyes. "Well—no. I . . ."

Her face flushed crimson. Suddenly it dawned on her what the chief was getting at. He suspected Brad of killing Jeremy!

"Brad didn't do it," she said in a desperate tone. "He wouldn't do something like that."

Danridge nodded sympathetically. "I'm not accusing anyone, Kelly. I just want to get the facts straight."

"Brad's innocent, I tell you!"

"Sure. You can go, Kelly. Tell Brad I want to see him again."

For a moment, Kelly considered telling the truth. She stood up slowly, hesitating in front of the desk. What if Brad had done something to Jeremy? No, he wasn't capable of murder. And it was Kelly's duty to protect him.

"Was there something else you wanted to tell me, Kelly?"

She turned toward the door. "No."

Kelly left the office, running straight into Brad's arms. "He wants to see you," she whispered. "He thinks you did it."

Brad withdrew from the embrace. "No way. I was backstage with Paul. Then I came out to find you."

She peered into his eyes. "I'll wait here for you."

Brad grimaced like an arrow had been shot through his heart. "Uh, Kelly, Mom and Dad—" He gestured to the frowning man and woman who sat on the bench in the waiting room a few yards away. "They think we should cool it for a while.

They think it would be best if we didn't see each other right now."

Kelly stepped back, glaring at him. "What?"

Brad sighed. "Maybe they're right."

"But—"

"Things have been going pretty bad, Kelly, since we started dating, I mean. You have to admit that—"

"No, I don't have to admit anything!"

"Kelly, it's just temporary, until this is settled."

She felt tired, angry, hurt. She didn't want to lose her temper. It just happened that way.

"It's only temporary," Brad said again.

"You used me!" Kelly cried. "You don't care about me. You're no better than the others."

The hurt was evident in his eyes. "No, Kelly, please—" He reached out for her, to hold her again.

Kelly gave him a violent shove. "Don't you touch me!"

"Kelly, I still love you."

"Well, I hate you!" she cried. "I hate you! I wish you were the one who had died!"

Everyone heard them fighting. Several of the law officers made a mental note of Kelly's hostile words. Chief Danridge had heard her in his office. Kelly did not realize what she had said.

Brad reached out again. "Kelly, please—"

She slapped his hand away. "Forget it! If you want to break up, fine. I hate you, Brad. Do you hear me? I hate you forever!"

Everyone in the station watched as Kelly ran

for the front door, fleeing from the horror into the coolness of the night. Brad stared after her for a moment, then went into the Chief's office for his interrogation.

Kelly lay on her bed for a long time that night, her glazed eyes staring at the ceiling of her bedroom. She had run home all the way from the police station. She found the house on MacDonald Avenue to be dark and empty. Her aunt had gone out for the evening, leaving Kelly a note on the refrigerator to say that she might be late. Kelly had retired immediately to the depressing solitude of her room, trying to sort out everything that had happened.

Someone had murdered Jeremy *after* she left the poolhouse. But who? Kelly knew she hadn't killed him, but everyone else was a suspect. Including Brad. Could Brad murder someone in cold blood? Kelly didn't think so.

As the clock struck one o'clock downstairs, Kelly heard the front door open and close. She sat up in her bed. Aunt Doris had arrived and was walking up the stairs. The footsteps halted in front of Kelly's door.

"Kelly, are you awake?"

Did Aunt Doris know about the murder? She'd have to find out sooner or later. She might as well hear it from Kelly.

"I'm awake, Aunt Doris, come on in."

But as soon as her aunt entered the room, Kelly

found herself unable to utter a word about the unfortunate incident in the pool dome.

"I saw your light," Aunt Doris said, slurring her words in a tipsy state. "How was the dance?"

Kelly shrugged. "Okay, I guess." How much did she know?

Steadying herself against the door, Doris Hendricks glared at Kelly. "I heard there was some kind of trouble at the gym. Were you involved in any of that?"

"The police talked to me," Kelly replied. "A boy had an accident in the swimming pool. He's dead."

"Is Brad all right?"

Kelly hesitated. "Uh, yes, he's fine."

She didn't have the strength to tell her aunt about the breakup. It was horrible enough to relive it in her mind, over and over, like some recurring nightmare. The truth would surface eventually, but Kelly would keep quiet tonight.

Aunt Doris waved at her. "Let me know if you need any help from me."

"Thanks."

"You're a good girl, Kelly. I know you didn't do anything wrong. Don't worry, it will all blow over."

I hope so, Kelly thought.

"Good night, Kelly."

She shuffled drunkenly down the hall, going into her bedroom.

Kelly's head hit the pillow again. She tossed and turned until daybreak, finally passing out as the rays of the sun hit her window. She slept most of the day, writhing with tortured dreams of what had happened. She saw herself in jail, separated from Brad forever.

"No!"

She sat up on her bed, sweat pouring from her face. She was not in jail. It was Saturday afternoon. She turned on her radio, listening to the news of Jeremy's demise. The football game had been cancelled because of the death at Central Academy. There had also been a bad car accident at the river. Then she listened to the weather forecast.

"Kelly?"

A light tapping on her door came behind the voice.

"I'm okay, Aunt Doris."

The door opened and Rachel stepped in. "It's me. I thought you might like to talk."

Kelly began to cry hysterically.

"I can leave if you want me to," Rachel offered.

Kelly stood up, unable to speak. She embraced Rachel. She needed a friend now more than ever.

Rachel wore a dire expression. She hated to bring more bad news, but Kelly had to know. And it was better that she heard it from her best friend.

"Kelly, listen to me—"

Kelly wiped her eyes. "I'm sorry, Rachel. It was so horrible. Just horrible. The police think Brad killed Jeremy. We broke up last night."

Rachel sighed. "Kelly, I came to talk to you about Brad."

"Talk about what?"

"Brad had an accident this morning. He's in the hospital."

Kelly drew back. "No! I must be dreaming. This isn't real."

Rachel grabbed her shoulders. "You're not dreaming. I'm sorry to be the one to tell you, but Brad's car crashed into the river this morning. He's in a coma."

"No!" Kelly cried. "It can't be."

"I couldn't believe it either," Rachel replied. "The news is on the radio, but they haven't released Brad's name. Marshall told me about it. He has a friend who works at the hospital."

Kelly reached for her denim jacket. "I have to see him. I have to go to the hospital."

"I'll take you," Rachel offered. "My mom said I could use the car."

"Hurry," Kelly said. "Before it's too late."

She had to get to Brad. Someone had hurt him. Kelly was sure of it. She had to be with him. She had to protect him as long as he was still alive.

TWELVE

When Kelly and Rachel arrived at Port City
Community Hospital, they had to wait a half hour
just to find out where Brad was. Even then, they
were not allowed to go into his cubicle in the
intensive care unit. Kelly had to stand in front of
the shatterproof glass window, peering helplessly
at her ex-boyfriend.

Brad was hooked up to several life-support
machines. His head had been wrapped in white
bandages. He was in a coma, the sleep of death.
Kelly had learned that translation in Latin class.
Brad might never wake up.

Kelly tapped on the thick glass. "Brad? Brad,
can you hear me?"

Rachel put her hand on Kelly's shoulder. "Come
on, there's nothing we can do. We'd better leave."

Kelly pulled away from her. "I've got to go in
there. Brad, wake up, it's me, Kelly. I love you,
Brad."

A severe-looking nurse appeared behind them.

"I'm afraid I'll have to ask you girls to leave if you can't hold it down."

Kelly turned to her. "Please, just let me see him for a minute."

"Only his mother and father are allowed in there. They'll be here soon, so I suggest you leave now."

Kelly didn't want to see Brad's mother and father. "Yes, you're right. Maybe I should go."

She clung to Rachel as they headed to the elevator. Kelly thought she was going to die from the agony. How could Jeremy be dead? How could Brad be lying there in a coma? It was all her fault.

When the elevator door opened, Victor Danridge stepped out to make things worse. "Kelly," he said, frowning. "I thought you might be here. I need to talk to you again. Your friend had better stay here."

Danridge led Kelly to a waiting room adjacent to the elevators. Kelly sat down in a cushioned chair. She still wasn't ready to tell the law officer the whole truth about Jeremy. She was afraid the truth might incriminate her.

"Kelly, what did you do after you left the police station last night?"

"I went home."

"Did you stay there all night?"

Kelly nodded. "My aunt came in around one. We talked. She went to bed but I couldn't fall asleep until dawn."

He raised an eyebrow. "We can check that."

"Go ahead. My aunt works downstairs in the hospital kitchen."

Danridge leaned back, and made a note. "Do you know anything about cars, Kelly? Anything at all?"

"Cars?" She was baffled by the question. "No, I don't have a car. I just got my driver's license this summer. Why?"

"We think someone might have cut the brake line in Brad's car. His brakes failed. That's why he crashed into the river."

"Are you sure?"

Danridge nodded. "Kelly, everyone saw you have that fight with Brad at the police station last night. I heard you tell them that you wished he was the one who had died—"

"No, I didn't mean it, sir. I swear. I didn't want to hurt Brad. It was our first fight. I love him. I—"

"All right, then. You can go. Unless you have something else you want to tell me?"

Kelly shook her head, lowering her eyes to the floor. She didn't have anything to say to the police. When she finally unburdened her soul, she would tell everything to Rachel.

"Rachel, I pushed Jeremy into the swimming pool."

Kelly was sitting on the edge of her bed. It was Sunday morning. Rachel had spent the night at Kelly's request because Kelly didn't want to be alone. They had been talking about Brad and Jeremy when Kelly blurted out the truth.

"You what?" Rachel asked, dumbfounded.

Kelly took a deep breath. "I pushed Jeremy into the pool." She told Rachel the entire story from start to finish.

Rachel whistled and shook her head in disbelief. "Wow. So Jeremy was alive when you left him."

"Yes, he was standing in the shallow end. He was wet but still alive. I thought he deserved a dunking after everything he had done to me."

Rachel took a step toward her. "Kelly, you have to tell the police."

"I can't, Rachel. They'll think I killed Jeremy. But it wasn't me. Someone came into the pool dome and killed him after I left."

Rachel rubbed her chin. "Unless it was an accident."

"I thought that too," Kelly replied. "But Chief Danridge thinks Jeremy was killed by a blow from a blunt instrument. And Chief Danridge told me that someone had cut the brake line on Brad's car. That's how he ended up in the river."

Rachel shivered through her entire body. "*Déjà vu.*"

"What?"

"Your parents, Kelly. Isn't that how they died? Their brakes failed and they went off the mountain."

Kelly shuddered at the macabre coincidence. She had to be the unluckiest girl in the world. She was always losing people who were near and dear to her. She prayed that Brad wouldn't be the next to die.

"Who would want to hurt Brad?" Rachel wondered.

Kelly sighed. "I don't—wait a minute! Liza! It has to be her."

"You think so?"

Kelly got off the bed, pacing up and down. "It makes perfect sense. She thinks Brad was the one who killed Jeremy. It's just like her to take revenge."

"Maybe—"

"I'm sure of it!"

But Rachel wasn't so certain. "Kelly, do you really think Liza knows enough about cars to do something like that? I mean, she doesn't even like to get her hands dirty in art class."

"It has to be her, Rachel! Who else could it be?"

Rachel shivered again. "Ugh. Liza, a killer."

"She was there when Brad and Jeremy fought," Kelly went on. "And she's done dirty stuff to me before. I'm pretty sure she knows that Jeremy was attracted to me. I—I could be next."

Rachel grabbed Kelly's arm. "You have to go to Chief Danridge."

"I can't."

"Kelly! Can't you see it? If Liza is a psycho, she's bound to come after you. You need protection."

"Not from the police. If I go to them, they'll think I hurt Brad and Jeremy. Liza will be off the hook for good."

Rachel threw out her hands. "Okay, then you tell me what we're going to do?"

"Get something on Liza. We have to get some

evidence that proves she hurt Brad. She could've killed Jeremy too. She was jealous of me. She could be working to make me look like the killer."

"Yeah," Rachel offered. "So far she's done a good job. But how will we turn it back on her?"

"Think," Kelly replied. "There must be a way."

They schemed for the rest of the day but they came up empty. Rachel kept insisting that Kelly go to the police, but Kelly would not relent. She knew that she had the best chance of catching Liza. Liza wouldn't be expecting Kelly to come after her. They just needed a plan.

Rachel agreed in spirit, but she was really afraid. They were on dangerous ground. What if Kelly was the next one to get hurt? If Liza was a psycho, Kelly had to be high on her list of victims.

It seemed hopeless to Rachel.

And it wouldn't get any better at school on Monday.

The next morning, Kelly and Rachel were walking to school on Rockbury Lane when the car pulled up behind them. The boys' voices rose in the cool September air. They weren't so flattering this time.

"Hey, killer girl! You slay me!"

"Don't 'brake' my heart, babe."

"How about a swim, honey!"

Kelly shuddered and her face reddened as the car screeched past them. "How do they know so much?"

"They heard your name in the gym Friday night," Rachel replied. "And they know about Jeremy and Brad. The rumor mill has been grinding all weekend. Are you sure you're up for this?"

"I hope so," Kelly replied.

But things were no better once she got to school. Everyone except Rachel stayed away from Kelly, avoiding her like a leper. Whenever she walked down the hall, she could hear them laughing and whispering behind her back. It returned her to the time when she was a fat girl. Now she was the object of ridicule for an entirely different reason. Someone had written the word "Killer" on her locker door. It was scrawled in bright, red Magic Marker.

The faculty wouldn't leave her alone either. Miss Monica called her in for a special counselling session. Kelly thought she was just trying to get a confession out of her, so she didn't say a word.

Mr. Kinsley also invited her into his office. He questioned her but Kelly refused to talk. Kinsley ended the conversation by asking her not to attend the memorial ceremony for Jeremy.

By the final bell, Kelly was sinking fast. She hadn't even been able to keep an eye on Liza, because Liza had stayed home. Brad's empty desk had made her cry. The day had been a complete disaster. At least until she met Rachel to walk home.

"It was the worst day of my life," Kelly told her.

"It was just like before, when everyone hated me."

Rachel glanced sideways at her friend. "You can still go to the police."

Kelly shook her head vehemently. "No."

They crossed the school grounds, heading down Rockbury Lane. Kelly's heart broke again when kids in a passing car shouted hateful comments. Everything had changed for the worse. But it didn't matter, not as long as Brad was still alive in the hospital. Kelly didn't care about being popular anymore.

"I miss him, Rachel. You can't imagine how much I miss him."

Rachel stopped in the middle of the sidewalk. "Kelly, are you ready to put an end to all of this?"

Kelly stopped beside her. "What are you talking about?"

"Do you want to fix Liza? To find out if she really is the one who hurt Brad and killed Jeremy?"

"She did it," Kelly replied. "I'm sure. I mean, she didn't even show her face in school today."

"So you're serious about wanting to show her up?"

"You know I am, Rachel."

Rachel started walking again. "Okay, then you have to listen to me. I've been thinking about it all day—"

Kelly followed her best friend toward the park. "What're you—"

"Just listen," Rachel replied, "I think I have a plan."

"A plan?"

"Yes, Kelly. And I'm pretty sure it will work. But you have to help me. I can't do it by myself."

Kelly told Rachel that she was ready for anything.

THIRTEEN

"I still say this is a stupid idea, Rachel."

Kelly sat in the front seat of the old Dodge Dart that Rachel had borrowed from her cousin in Rochester. They were cruising the streets of Port City on a Saturday night. It was all part of Rachel's master plan. They had taken a whole week to set it up correctly. But after two days in motion, Kelly had little faith that the ploy would work.

"In the past two days, we've been all over the county," Kelly went on. "And nothing—*nothing*—has happened."

"Give it time, Kelly."

Rachel was behind the wheel of the Dart, steering the vehicle past Central Academy once again. In her disguise, Rachel looked entirely different. Part of the plan involved Rachel dressing up like a boy. She wore a man's long-sleeved shirt, straight-legged jeans, and black running shoes. Her hair had been tucked under a Rochester High baseball cap. In the dim light of evening, Rachel passed easily for a male.

"It doesn't look good," Kelly said. "Rachel, are you listening?"

Rachel sighed. "Kelly, we've come too far to quit now."

"I just don't think it's going to work," Kelly insisted.

"Do you have any better ideas?" Rachel asked testily.

Kelly grew quiet, considering the elaborate details that had been implemented in the scheme. First, they had to convince everyone at Central that Kelly had begun to date a jock from Rochester High. It had to be a boy from another school so no one would be able to identify him. As the rumors grew, the senior class began to believe that Kelly had chosen a new boyfriend with Brad still lying in a coma at the hospital. As soon as the story was firmly set in the minds of the students, they began to lay the groundwork for the next part of the plan.

Rachel glanced sideways at Kelly. "Lean a little closer to me. We need to make it look real."

Kelly grimaced. "This is ridiculous."

"You want it to look legit, don't you?"

Kelly gave in, leaning closer like a girl in love. She wished she could have more confidence in Rachel's strategy. The basic idea was to draw out Liza by making her think that Kelly had a new boyfriend. Liza would be so jealous of Kelly's happiness that she was sure to come after them, seeking revenge the way she had done with Jeremy and Brad.

On Friday night, they had faked the first "date" by taking in a movie and going for burgers afterward. They made sure that some of Liza's cheerleader friends saw them from a distance. Even though they seemed to believe the ruse, so far Liza had not made a move.

"Maybe it isn't Liza at all," Kelly offered as they rolled along Middle Road. "Maybe it was somebody else."

"Like who?"

"I don't know. What about Marshall? He's smart. And he was really jealous of Brad."

Rachel shook her head. "Marshall's a wimp. He could never do something like that. He doesn't have it in him."

Their Saturday "date" had been an all-day affair. Starting early that morning, they drove up to Thunder Lake for a picnic. But when Liza didn't show herself, they headed back to Port City, hitting every tourist stop and local attraction, keeping a high profile so everyone could see the heartless Kelly with her new beau. Still no results.

When darkness came, they went to another movie, again spotted by Liza's haughty group, who laughed and pointed in Kelly's direction. But no Liza. After they left the theater, they drove around town, keeping their eyes open for a flash of bleached-blond hair.

"Face it, Rachel, this isn't going to work."

Rachel grimaced. "Maybe you're right. I'm tired of dressing like this."

"What time is it?"

"Almost ten."

"Ride by the house," Kelly told her. "I want to see if my aunt is home yet."

Reluctantly, Rachel headed for Pitney Docks. She wondered if they had overestimated Liza's anger. Maybe Liza was lying low, waiting for a better opening. How long would Liza wait before she came after Kelly?

As the Dodge pulled onto MacDonald Street, Kelly glanced toward the dark townhouse. Aunt Doris wasn't home from her evening of drinking. Her aunt didn't seem to care one whit about Kelly's problems.

"You want to call it a night?" Rachel asked.

Kelly shook her head. "No, keep going. We don't have anything else to do. I can't see Brad until visiting hours tomorrow."

Kelly had been to the hospital every day since the accident, peering sadly through the glass wall. Somehow, she thought Brad would wake up if she could just talk to him. Maybe her sweet words would bring him out of the coma.

At the end of the street, Rachel made a U-turn, heading back toward Taylor Street. As soon as she turned right to follow the edge of the park, a pair of bright headlights hit the Dodge. The car immediately pulled away from the curb, coming up behind them.

Rachel glanced at the rearview mirror. "Somebody's following us."

Kelly shrugged. "Probably nobody we know."

"He's staying close on our tail."

Kelly looked back for a moment but she couldn't see the driver. "Turn right when you get to Pleasant Street. Go away from town, see what happens."

They were unconcerned as Rachel made the turn. But the bright headlights swung in their direction, staying directly behind them. The car was following the two girls, who immediately began to worry.

"I can't believe it worked," Rachel said. "Can you see anything?"

Kelly shook her head. "No, I can't tell—my God, the car is red!"

Rachel's face grew pale. "Jeremy had a red car."

"No! It can't be. Nobody can come back from the dead. Take the next right."

As Rachel made the turn, she regretted her plan. She had wanted to draw out Jeremy's killer, but now, with the car on their tail, the idea seemed foolish. Their plan had worked too well.

"He's still there!" Kelly said nervously.

Rachel's hands had turned bone-white on the steering wheel. "I'm going to try to lose him. Hang on, I hope this bucket of bolts can stand the strain."

The Dodge shook and rattled as Rachel gunned the throttle. They pulled away from the red car, tires squealing as they sped out of the city limits, heading for the beach. As soon as they took the first winding turn, the red car's headlights disappeared for a moment.

"I think he gave up," Kelly offered.

Rachel's eyes lifted for a second to the mirror. "I hope so. The only thing out here is Lighthouse Point. There's no place for us to go unless we turn back or go to the Coast Guard station."

They glanced at the temperature gauge on the dashboard. The needle was driving over into the "Hot" zone. The car was too old to race down the highway, but Rachel had no other choice. She had to outrun the red car.

Kelly gazed over her shoulder again. "Oh no." The red car was still following them and it seemed to be gaining.

"Kelly, what are we going to do?"

"Can you go any faster?"

Rachel pressed the accelerator to the floor. "Here goes nothing!"

They didn't hear the hissing under the hood as a water hose split.

"Kelly!"

"Okay, okay. Stay calm. We can follow Beach Road past Lighthouse Point."

"But that's the way to the Coast Guard station."

The red car's lights flashed in Kelly's hazel eyes. "That's fine with me. Go faster."

The Dodge outdistanced the red car for another mile before they saw the entrance to Lighthouse Point. Kelly hoped other cars would be there on a Saturday night, but the parking lot was empty. It didn't matter. They could find help at the Coast Guard station. Surely the killer would not come after them there.

"Is he still there?" Rachel asked.

"I don't see him. Maybe it isn't—"

Something clunked under the hood of the Dodge. Steam began to pour out of the engine. Suddenly the Dodge started to slow down. The engine died at the entrance to Lighthouse Point Park.

An expression of sheer terror had frozen Rachel's thin face. "What are we going to do?"

Kelly opened her door. "Get out."

"But—"

"Just do it!"

They jumped out into the road. Kelly gazed back at the lights burning on the dark highway. The red car was racing toward them, rushing forward like some monster with glowing eyes.

"Maybe he's not after us," Rachel offered as she also peered at the lights.

"We can't take any chances. Head for the platform on the observation deck."

"Kelly—"

"Hurry!"

They fled across the empty parking lot, running in the direction of the observation deck. The beam of the lighthouse circled over the rough waters of the Atlantic, putting an eerie sheen on the white-capped waves. Black clouds were forming over the ocean to blot the stars and the moon. A squall was pushing in from the east, riding the edge of a stiff wind.

When they reached the concrete steps that led up to the observation deck, Rachel had to stop to catch her breath. "I can't run anymore. My side hurts."

Kelly gazed up at the platform. "We have to climb."

Rachel raised her head. "We'll be trapped up there."

"No, we can climb down the other side, to the beach."

"Kelly—"

"If we hide in the rocks, he'll never be able to find us."

"Or she," Rachel said.

"I don't care, we have to hide."

Rachel grabbed her arm. "Kelly, what if it is Liza? There's only one of her and two of us. We can overpower her."

"Do you want to take that chance?" Kelly asked grimly.

They gazed back toward the steaming Dodge. The red car had arrived, stopping next to the stranded vehicle for a moment. They held their breath, praying that the red car would move on toward the Coast Guard station. Maybe it was one of the seamen going to work.

The red car swerved around the Dodge and entered the empty parking lot. It was coming straight for them. The headlights blinded Kelly for a moment.

"Maybe he just wants to help us," Rachel said.

"I don't want to find out the hard way," Kelly replied. "Hurry, let's get on the other side before it's too late."

Rachel wasn't in the mood to argue.

As they climbed the steps, they could hear the waves crashing against the rocks below them. The beam from the lighthouse washed over the platform, illuminating the stairwell for a second. A beacon to light their way, Kelly thought morbidly—the way to their graves!

When they reached the top of the platform, Kelly turned back to look at the red car. It had stopped in the parking lot, switching off the bright headlights. The door opened on the passenger side. A dark figure climbed out, closing the door, moving toward the platform. In the dim light, Kelly couldn't tell if the person was male or female.

Rachel held her aching side. "Kelly—"

Kelly turned her toward the set of stairs on the opposite side. "Come on, we can make it to the rocks in time to hide."

"I can't run."

"You have to, Rachel."

The surface of the platform was slick with sea spray. They had to move slowly to keep from slipping. When they got to the other side of the deck, Kelly started down the steps first.

Rachel came right behind her. But she didn't hold on to the handrail. She tripped on the second step and lost her balance. She screamed as she tumbled into Kelly, twisting on the wet stairs.

Kelly turned in time to catch Rachel, but she almost fell herself. They teetered there until Kelly grabbed the handrail. Rachel sank to the steps, holding her ankle. Kelly tried to get Rachel to her feet but Rachel could not put any weight on her left leg. She yelped in pain.

"I think it's broken!" Rachel cried.

The ray of the lighthouse swept over them. Kelly saw the blood seeping from Rachel's leg. She attempted to carry Rachel down the steps but it was too awkward.

They were trapped there.

Kelly eased Rachel onto the steps. Rachel bit back a scream when she saw the blood oozing on her skin. Kelly sat next to her, wondering how long it would be until their pursuer was upon them.

"Save yourself!" Rachel told her.

Kelly shook her head. "I'm going to fight. I need something to use as a weapon." But there was nothing handy.

"Maybe she'll fall on the other steps," Rachel said bitterly.

Kelly sat up straight. Of course, that was it. She could wait for the intruder to start down the beachside stairs, then they could trip their tormentor and send the demon into the rocks below.

"Can you move down a couple of steps?" she asked Rachel.

Rachel moaned but she managed to lower herself a few feet.

"Now hold on to the railing," Kelly told her. "And watch out. I'm going to trip him."

Kelly climbed up again, peering over the edge of the platform. The light circled three times before the dark figure stepped onto the deck. For a moment, the intruder hesitated, stopping on the slick surface.

But then the light swung around, flashing on a face that Kelly recognized immediately. "My God!"

"What is it?" Rachel hissed.

Kelly stood up. "It's Aunt Doris."

What was her aunt doing out here? Where had she gotten a car? And why had she followed them all the way from Port City?

Kelly moved in the direction of her aunt, waving wildly. "Aunt Doris! Over here. Thank God. I thought you were—"

The light shined on her aunt again.

Doris Hendricks stood at the edge of the platform, staring at Kelly. She wore her white hospital uniform. Her face was pale and haggard in the harsh brightness of the beam from the lighthouse.

"Aunt Doris, you have to take us back to town!" Kelly cried.

"I don't have to do anything!" her aunt replied, viciously.

Kelly stopped in the middle of the observation deck. She waited for the light again. This time the beam revealed the small sledgehammer that her aunt held in her right hand.

Kelly knew then that her aunt had not come to help them.

FOURTEEN

Doris Hendricks's free hand closed around the handle of the sledgehammer. She came at Kelly in a slow, deliberate motion, holding the hammer like an ax, stalking her wide-eyed niece. The beam of light kept sweeping over them, burning like the fires of the underworld.

Kelly began to walk backward. She moved to her left, away from Rachel. They were both going to die if Kelly didn't do something to save them.

"I fooled you!" her aunt cried. "I fooled everyone. You never knew it was me."

Kelly could not believe what she was seeing and hearing. "Aunt Doris, what are you—"

"It's over for you, Kelly! Just like it was over for your mother."

"Mom?"

A wicked, cackling sound escaped from the mouth of her aunt. "You never knew it was me. I fixed them. I rigged their brakes so they'd go off

159

that mountain. You were at camp, so you never suspected me."

"You killed Mom and Dad?"

"And your boyfriend Jeremy, too! I've been following you, Kelly, you little tramp. I was there at the dance when you went into the poolhouse with that boy. I know what you were doing in there! But I put a stop to it. I made sure he'd never touch you again."

"No, you're wrong. Jeremy wasn't my boyfriend."

Her aunt didn't seem to understand. "They were all your boyfriends! But I fixed them. Just like I fixed that tramp mother of yours!"

Kelly felt the safety railing, damp and cold against her back. She began to slide along the railing, following it to the other end of the platform. Aunt Doris kept coming, ready with her weapon.

"You cut the brake line on Brad's car!" Kelly accused.

Her aunt laughed maniacally. "Yes, I did his brakes. Just like your mother!"

"Those notes. You left them for me. And the phone calls. You were the one who—"

Kelly's feet suddenly slipped out from under her on the wet surface of the deck. She felt herself falling. She caught the railing, which kept her from going over the side, from crashing on the rocks below.

"Fool!"

Aunt Doris lunged at her with the hammer.

Kelly managed to roll to the side, barely escaping the blow. The hammer slammed into the railing. A stinging sensation spread through her aunt's hands, stopping her for a moment.

Kelly used the railing to pull herself to her feet again. "You're sick, Aunt Doris. You need help."

"No, I'm not crazy. I'm sane. And you won't escape me, Kelly. I'm going to kill you. Then I'll kill your friend. And guess what? I'll enjoy it as much as I enjoyed killing your mother."

Kelly stared at her through the mist of the sea spray, horrified by the admission. "Why? Why did you kill my parents?"

The lighthouse beam revealed the anguished expression on her aunt's face. "Your mother! She was my sister, but she was a tramp, just like you. But my mother thought she was the good one, the pretty one. And I was nothing, the ugly duckling. She was horrible to me!"

"No, that's not true. Mom was a good person. You're the—"

"She stole my boyfriends! She stole your father from me. He was *mine* before she came along. He was my boyfriend first!"

"That's impossible!" Kelly cried. "Mom met Dad in New York, while she was on vacation. She talked him into moving to Port City. He never even knew you back then."

"Liar! You're just like her. I knew he loved me, but she took him from me!"

"Aunt Doris, please—"

"I kept you fat and ugly, Kelly. I made you wear

cheap clothes and those stupid glasses. You were hideous, just the way I wanted you."

Kelly kept moving along the rail, inching to the opposite end of the deck. "You did that to me on purpose?"

"Everything was perfect. But then you had to change. And I had to stop you. I wasn't going to let it happen again. I wasn't going to let you steal my boyfriends the way my sister did."

Kelly scowled at her. "You don't have any boyfriends!"

"Hah! That's what you think. I have a lot of boyfriends. I see them every day—"

"In bars?"

"Yes! I'd never bring them home. I never wanted them to see the fat leech who sucked me dry."

Kelly bumped into the barrier at the far edge of the platform. There was no more room for her to run. She had to go around her aunt—or through her. She knew that Doris Hendricks was beyond listening to reason.

"You have to die, Kelly."

"Stay away from me!"

Her aunt crept closer, holding the hammer in front of her. "You can't know how much I hate you, Kelly. I would've had a husband if you hadn't been on my back. What luck! I kill your mother to get rid of her and the court awards me custody of an eight-year-old brat. And you look just like her. That's why I made sure you were fat. You aren't going to steal my boyfriends."

"If you hate me so much, why did you take care of me?" Kelly asked, her emotions churning. "Why didn't you give me up for adoption?"

"I wanted to ruin you myself. I was going to kill you eventually, but I had to keep you alive until you turned eighteen so I could get the rest of the money."

"Money?"

"It doesn't matter now, Kelly. I'm don't care about the money anymore. I just want you out of the way! Good-bye, my dear niece. I'll see you in hell!"

She lifted the hammer over her head. The lighthouse sent a reflection off the smooth hammerhead. She rushed at Kelly, screeching madly.

Kelly tensed against the railing, using it to launch herself toward her attacker. She caught her aunt's wrists, stopping the weapon from reaching its target. They wrestled on the slick surface until her aunt pulled back from Kelly.

"You're strong," she said. "Stronger than I thought. But I'm even stronger."

She moved slowly this time, jabbing at Kelly, driving her back against the rail. The lighthouse kept turning, strobing the platform with its eerie light. Her aunt's face was there and then gone in the shadows, a hideous goblin smiling at all the wanton destruction.

The hammer swung sideways at Kelly. She reached out to block the blow. The peen hit her hand, shattering several bones. A sharp pain shot up Kelly's left arm. When Kelly dropped her hand, the hammer smashed into her left shoulder.

In desperation, Kelly rushed her aunt, using her superior weight to knock the older woman to the slick surface of the platform. Her aunt went limp as soon as she hit the deck. Kelly stood over her, trying to catch her breath. Kelly's chest ached as she drew air. Her hand throbbed and she was fairly certain that her shoulder had been dislocated. Her left arm hung loosely by her side, worthless for self-defense.

"Kelly!"

The faint echo rose above the sound of the waves. "Rachel!"

She took a step toward her fallen friend.

But her aunt cried out suddenly, lifting her head. She swung the hammer from her prone posture, catching Kelly in the shin. Kelly lurched to one side, falling in the middle of the platform. Her right leg went numb. She couldn't get up this time.

Aunt Doris leapt to her feet. "Fooled you, fooled you!" Her nasal voice came out in a singsong rhythm.

Kelly started to crawl away from her. Aunt Doris followed her slowly, grinning in the strobing beam. She circled Kelly, driving her niece to the ocean side of the observation platform. Kelly bumped against the safety rail. She could not crawl any further.

"Now you die!"

The hammer rose in the air. Kelly looked up into her doom. There was nothing she could do in her crippled state except put out her one good arm to deflect the blow. The hammer snapped her wrist, causing the arm to fall. Kelly knew the next strike would smash her skull.

Doris Hendricks steadied herself for the death blow. Her eyes were orbs of insanity as she lifted the weapon. At that moment, her irises caught the full intensity of the flashing ray from the lighthouse. She screamed and lowered the hammer.

"I'm blind! I'm blind!"

She began to turn in circles, unable to see anything.

Kelly perceived the small opening. She started to crawl, pushing herself along the deck, keeping her back to the platform. Despite the agony of her wounds, the going was easy on the slippery surface.

"I'm going to kill you," her aunt cried. "Where are you?"

"You can't see me!" Kelly hollered. "You don't know where I am."

"I'm going to beat you to death!"

"Here I am, Aunt Doris! Over here. Can't you see me? I'm right in front of your stupid face."

Her aunt turned in a complete circle before she was able to fix the direction of Kelly's voice.

Kelly just kept crawling, scooting on her backside. She was heading for the steps. She wondered if she could make it to Rachel before her aunt regained her sight.

"Here I am! Come and get me!"

Her aunt began to stumble forward. She found the railing and started in Kelly's direction. But Kelly didn't care. She was almost to the steps. She could hear Rachel's cries more clearly now.

"I don't care about the money," her aunt cried wildly. "The child must not live. Must not live!"

"Hey, Aunt Crazy, I'm right here. Keep coming!"

The madwoman stayed on the rail, holding the hammer in one hand, sliding in the direction of her niece's voice.

"You're almost on me!" Kelly cried. "Closer, closer."

"I can hear you. I can hear you!"

Kelly felt the opening of the stairwell behind her. She slid onto the steps, bumping a few times before Rachel stopped her. Rachel started to say something, but Kelly wouldn't let her speak.

"Here I am!" she cried again. "Now, Aunt Doris. Hit me now."

To the blind woman, it sounded like Kelly was directly beneath her. With an animalistic cry, Doris Hendricks lifted the hammer above her head. But when she brought it down, she struck nothing but air. She lost her balance, tumbling forward. But instead of falling down the stairs, she went over the handrail, plummeting to the rocks below with a bloodcurdling scream.

"My God!" Rachel whispered.

Kelly had to make sure. She crawled to the bannister, peering down into the turbulent water. At first, she could not see anything in the darkness.

But then the lighthouse beam swung over the beach again. Kelly caught a glimpse of her aunt's body lying in the water. Doris Hendricks had bounced against the rocks, crashing headfirst like a crushed flower in the tide.

Kelly lay back on the steps, closing her eyes.

It was a long time before someone saw the abandoned car and came to rescue them.

Chief Victor Danridge sat beside Kelly's hospital bed with a notebook in his hand. He had been conducting his investigation for four days. After her surgery, Kelly told him everything with Rachel corroborating as much as she could. Kelly wasn't sure that Danridge believed her.

He glanced up from his notes, smiling. "How do you feel?"

"Lousy," Kelly replied.

Both of her arms and one leg were in plaster casts. The cast on her left arm went all the way to her shoulder, the site of her operation. The doctors were certain she would recover at least ninety percent of her shoulder's full capacity. She was going to be fine—physically.

"I'm going to miss a lot of school," she said meekly.

"You'll make it up in no time," Danridge replied pleasantly. "I've already spoken to Miss

Monica. She's agreed to act as your temporary guardian. And Coach Sikes is looking for a tutor for you."

She perked up a little. "Really? Then you're not going to arrest me?"

He laughed lightheartedly. "No. I believe your story, Kelly. We found Jeremy Rice's blood on a blouse in your aunt's bedroom."

Kelly exhaled defeatedly. "Oh." Her aunt had ruined so many lives.

"Kelly, why did you and your aunt live in Pitney Docks?"

Her brow wrinkled. "We were poor."

"No, you weren't."

Chief Danridge went on to explain how there were three savings accounts at Port City Savings Bank in the name of Kelly Ann Langdon, with Aunt Doris listed as the guardian of the trust. The balances of the accounts totaled over four hundred thousand dollars. There was also a checking account in the name of Doris Hendricks, balance twenty-five thousand, four hundred thirty dollars and eighty-one cents.

"It has to be a mistake," Kelly told him. "We never had a dime."

Danridge shifted anxiously in the chair. "Your father was an engineer at the shipyard, Kelly. He built a stock portfolio that's also in your trust. Most of the money in the savings accounts came from his life insurance. It was stipulated in his will that your aunt could spend the interest on the trust, but she couldn't touch any of the principal unless it was spent on you."

"But she had a job at the hospital."

"No, she was a volunteer there. She just did that to make you think she was working. In the meantime, she was using the interest on the trust to hang out in some of the local bars. She was skimming, Kelly, holding out on you. She kept a car in a garage a few blocks away. She never even let you know she had it."

Kelly nodded slowly, a glow of recognition bringing her face to life. "That's what she meant by the money. When we were at the beach, she said that she didn't care about the money anymore."

"Do you have any idea what made her snap?"

Kelly closed her eyes, trying not to cry. Her body hurt when she cried. She didn't want to hurt anymore.

"She hated my mother," Kelly replied. "She killed her. She got weird after I lost a lot of weight. She said I looked just like my mother. I guess I reminded her of what she had done."

"It's over, Kelly. And you're a rich girl."

The tears came anyway, dragging her over the bumpy road. "I don't feel very rich."

Danridge stood up and snapped his fingers. "I think there's somebody who'd like to say hello to you. Rachel, bring him in."

Rachel limped through the door, pushing a wheelchair.

Kelly's eyes grew wide when she saw the occupant of the chair.

It was Brad.

He had awakened from his coma to smile at her.

He was alive and wanted to talk to his girlfriend.

EPILOGUE

Graduation Day was also Kelly's seventeenth birthday. She wore the red gown and the mortarboard with the red and white tassel, the school colors for Central Academy. Despite missing two months of her fall classes, Kelly had managed to graduate with honors. She finished third in the senior class, scoring well enough on her SATs to gain entrance to Dartmouth. She still wasn't sure if she wanted to go to an Ivy League school.

After the ceremony, she met Rachel and Rachel's mother outside the gym. Kelly had been living with them in a new house in Morningside Groves. Kelly was paying the rent from the interest on her trust. She still couldn't believe that the money was there, had always been there. Her aunt had been a greedy, hateful woman.

"We're high school graduates," Rachel said with mock pride. "And it's even your birthday. How do you want to celebrate?"

"Why don't I meet you back at the house?" Kelly replied. "I have to talk to Brad first."

Rachel winked at her best friend. She didn't envy Kelly at all. Rachel had won an academic scholarship to Wheaton College. They could still see each other on holidays.

"Come on, Mom."

Rachel's mother followed after her, remarking that Rachel should find a nice young man like Brad.

Kelly would drive herself home in her new Mazda Miata. Miss Monica had helped her get the car. Of course, Rachel was allowed to drive it whenever she wanted to.

Miss Monica had been great. She had doubled up on the counseling sessions during Kelly's recovery. It had been tough for a while.

It was still tough, Kelly thought.

She moved through the crowd, looking for Brad.

Kelly was afraid. Everything had moved so quickly. She was still a little dazed from the unfortunate events of the fall. Something like that took its toll. She still had dreams about her aunt, standing there in the spectral glow of the blinding light.

How could her aunt have been so cruel?

Kelly shuddered in the crowd. She was surrounded by people but she felt all alone in the world. Being wealthy didn't help the pain inside her, the aching and longing that came from wanting someone special.

"Kelly, over here!"

Brad was coming toward her through the crowd. He had already taken off his cap and gown. He looked so handsome.

Kelly had paid his hospital bills with her new-found wealth. His parents had initially resisted their getting back together, but Brad would not let them influence him. Kelly was his girl. He wouldn't have it any other way.

As she watched him moving toward her, Kelly realized how much she loved him. She wondered what would happen to them now that they were finished at Central. Would they drift apart like other high school sweethearts?

Of all her fears, the thought of losing Brad was the worst.

"Hi, beautiful," Brad said, touching her chin. "Graduates. Big deal. I don't feel any different."

Kelly smiled. "I've never kissed a high school graduate before, not on the lips anyway."

He wrapped his arms around her, pulling her close. "Oh, I think that can be arranged."

Their lips met and Kelly clung tightly to him like she never wanted to let go.

"Oh, Brad. I'm so scared."

He drew back, gazing into her hazel eyes. "What's wrong?"

She sighed. "What do we do now?"

He frowned. "I know what you mean."

"You do?"

"You're going to Dartmouth. But we have the summer."

She touched his cheek. "We don't have to break up at the end of the summer, Brad."

He shook his head sadly. "My parents can't afford to send me to Dartmouth, Kelly. Private school tuition is outrageous."

"I can afford to send you," Kelly replied.

"What?"

"Brad, I'll pay your tuition. I have the money. Why shouldn't you go to Dartmouth? It's a great school."

"Kelly, I couldn't take your money."

She leaned closer to him, whispering in his ear. "You could take my money if we were, well, married or something."

His face went slack. "Married?"

Kelly shrugged. "Why not? I love you, you love me. Why shouldn't we get married? After college, I mean."

"Kelly!"

"Brad! I love you."

A stunned, glassy looked appeared in his eyes. It was quickly replaced by a devilish grin. "Kelly, are you asking me to . . ."

"I guess I am, Brad," she said.

Brad was speechless.

So Kelly answered for him. With a kiss.

WELCOME TO TERROR ACADEMY . . .

It's like any other high school on the outside. But inside, fear stalks the halls — and terror is in a class by itself.

────────────

Please turn the page for a sneak preview of the next TERROR ACADEMY book — don't miss SPRING BREAK!

Laura Hollister lowered her dark brown eyes to the first question of her Honors English examination. As her pretty face bent toward the page, a lock of thick, black hair fell over her high cheekbones, blocking her vision for a moment. She brushed back the unruly tresses, sighing and frowning at the purple print that smelled of mimeograph toner. Laura had studied hard for the exam, but she didn't want to take it, even though it was the last test before spring break and signaled a temporary end to homework, pop quizzes, term papers and tardy bells. Unlike most of the students at Central Academy, Laura wasn't looking forward to spring break.

"Is something wrong, Miss Hollister?"

Laura glanced up to see her teacher, Mr. Frankland, staring at her. His sharp tone had forced everyone else in the class to look up at Laura. Mr. Frankland was Laura's least favorite teacher, though she pretended to like him because she didn't want him to be angry with her.

"Uh, no everything is fine, Mr. Frankland."

But he would not let it rest. "You know, Miss Hollister, that this test counts as half your grade for the second semester."

"Yes, sir."

"Then I suggest you get to work."

"Yes, sir."

She dropped her eyes to the paper again, a distressed expression on her pale face. Laura was an attractive girl with a short, upturned nose that gave her the appearance of snobbishness on first glance. But one smile on her full lips and her hearty laugh told anyone that she was usually a good-natured person. Today, however, she was filled with dread at the onset of the two-week hiatus that came every year at the end of March.

The first question was on *Julius Caesar*, the Shakespearian tragedy that they had read back in February.

Why did Brutus want to kill Caesar?

Laura wrote down, "To preserve the republic." She studied the answer for a moment, deciding it wasn't enough for Mr. Frankland, so she added, "Brutus feared the crowning of Caesar as emperor." That should do it, she thought.

Her intelligence took over, allowing Laura to forget her woeful musings. She began to breeze through the questions, her pencil blazing. Mr. Frankland always gave short answer and essay questions, preferring that format to multiple choice. Difficult classes were a fact of the honors program at Central, the best school in the Port City area. Anyone who graduated from Central Academy had a good chance of going on to a great college.

Laura reached the essay question before anyone else in the class. It was about *The Old Man and the Sea*, the short novel by Ernest Hemingway. Laura took her time answering the question but she was still finished with the exam in forty minutes, leaving twenty minutes until the bell rang. Even after she had rechecked her answers, a full fifteen minutes remained on the clock.

Laura sighed again and leaned back in her chair. Spring break loomed before her, a grim reminder of what was to come. How could they do this to her? She was sixteen! Soon to be seventeen, which meant that she was almost an adult. Didn't she have a say in the way she lived her own life?

Putting down the pencil, she let her eyes wander to the casement of the window. It was a dreary March day. A dull, gray sky formed an ugly ceiling over Port City. She could see gulls and terns riding the air currents as they swooped down toward the Tide Gate River. The sea birds were free, she thought, not a prisoner like *her*.

"Miss Hollister—"

She glared back at Mr. Frankland's soda-bottle glasses. "What!"

"Are you finished?"

She exhaled. "Yes!"

"Even the last question?" he challenged.

"Yes, the one about *The Old Man and the Sea*."

He laughed a little. "No, look on the back of the page."

Rolling her eyes impatiently, she flipped over the exam paper to see the question that was marked, *Just for Fun: What do you anticipate from your spring break?* Mr. Frankland was always trying to be amusing, though his "Just for Fun" questions were far from entertaining.

Laura blushed and tried to smile. "Oh, I'm sorry, I—"

"It's all right," he replied. "You still have ten minutes."

Laura knew she had to answer the question even though it was silly and, to her, horrifying. If she didn't attempt some kind of response, it might offend Mr. Frankland and thereby affect her final grade. She had a perfect average at Central. She didn't want to blow it just because she was in a bad mood.

What *do* I expect from my spring break? she wondered.

In an almost involuntary gesture, her pencil began to move, writing one word: *Disaster!*

No! That wouldn't do. It was the kind of response that would make him angry, force him to nitpick every one of her answers.

Disaster!

It was true enough. There had to be a way out of it. She couldn't let the answer stand though. She erased it and wrote something about enriching her studies at the library, even if that wasn't what lay ahead. It was the kind of thing that Mr. Frankland would buy, however.

The bell rang, ending the torment of one thing, beginning the torture of another. Laura slid out of her desk, moving toward Mr. Frankland. She knew she should apologize for the way she had been acting but she didn't feel like sucking up anymore. School was out for two weeks. She wouldn't have to sit in Mr. Frankland's class for a while. He'd forget her rudeness soon enough.

Laura dropped the test paper on his desk and headed for the door. When he called to her, she just kept going. She had other things on her mind. And they all spelled one word.

Disaster.

The halls of Central Academy were uncharacteristically wild and raucous with the onset of spring break. It was like some lunatic asylum had unleashed the inmates for a day of panic and chaos. Laura moved toward her locker, slogging between the joyous furor of her classmates. All of the juniors attended classes in the same building, one of three structures that housed the classrooms for grades nine through twelve.

Laura wished she could share in some of the merriment but the feeling just wasn't there. Sure, she looked like any other student in the junior class. She wore a hooded, blue parka over her jeans and Central Academy T-shirt, and stylish running shoes. With her tall, slender frame and cover-girl looks, she was one of the most sought after girls for Friday night dates. In spite of her boyfriend, Charlie, guys were always asking her out. How would she rid herself of the pain in her heart? It would take some kind of miracle to stop the aching.

Pausing in front of her locker, she put her head against the door and stood there, wishing that she could just die. Maybe there was a way. No, it was set. She was stuck with no escape.

Disaster!

Gloom and doom.

Misery to the max!

"Hey, gorgeous, what's with you?"

She felt a hand on her shoulder. Laura turned to look into the eyes of Charlie Sherwood, her boyfriend. His handsome face was all smiles and happiness, just like the other members of the junior class.

Laura sighed dejectedly. "Hi, Charlie."

"You don't look happy."

"I'm not."

"Maybe this will make you feel better."

He took her face in his hands, lowering his lips to her mouth for a sweet kiss. They had been going steady since Christmas. Charlie was a nice guy, and really cute with green eyes, sandy hair and a runner's build. He wasn't a jock, even though he ran cross-country for the Central track team. He also studied hard so he'd have the grades for college after graduation.

Laura broke away from the kiss. "Not now."

Charlie frowned. "What's wrong?"

"I don't know," she replied. "I'm just down."

Charlie laughed. "Down? This is the greatest. School's out. We're free. I love it, babe."

"I know, I know," Laura moaned.

"We've got two whole weeks together. It's gonna be hot. I'm stoked, Laura. You should be too."

She leaned back against the locker, trying to smile. Charlie was so sweet. She hadn't told him yet. She hadn't told anyone except her best friend, Kimmy. How was she going to break the news to the only boy she had ever loved? It might split them up forever when he found out.

Charlie put his hand on her soft cheek. "Laura, this is going to be special. You know what I mean? We've been talking about it all winter. You and me? You know . . ."

"Charlie, don't start with this right now, okay?"

"But I thought—"

"I *know* what you think. That's all you ever think about."

He pulled his hand away. "I love you, Laura. And I thought you loved me. You said you did."

Laura exhaled, making a defeated sound. "I *do* love you, Charlie. But I can't think about this right now. Okay?"

His green eyes narrowed into an expression of genuine concern. "What's wrong, babe?"

"Charlie . . ."

How was she going to tell him? Would it ruin everything? They had come so far together. Their relationship had been growing every day. Charlie had promised to give her a pre-engagement ring as soon as he got it from the jeweler.

"Laura, you can tell me anything. You know that."

"Charlie, I need time to think."

He took a step backward, grimacing in that impatient way boys had when they were confused by girls. "Think about what?"

Laura heard the voice in the back of her mind, articulating her worst fears. She saw the other girls descending on Charlie, taking him away from her. She heard their laughter, imagining Charlie as he chose the most beautiful girl in Port City. The girl who would give him exactly what he wanted!

"I'm not sure, Charlie. I mean, we're moving too fast. I think we should wait a while. Until we're more sure."

Charlie reached out again, stroking the long, black tresses that fell onto Laura's shoulders. "I *am* sure. I love you."

"Oh, Charlie, I love you too. But—"

His hand fell to his side. "But! It's always but! It's always going to be but! Isn't it?"

"Not forever," Laura replied.

How could she tell him what was *really* wrong? It didn't seem to matter. Either way he was going to be angry. She was ruining their spring break in a single moment.

Charlie took a deep breath, shaking his head. "I'm sorry, Laura. It's just, I get crazy when I'm with you. I've never felt like this about anyone. I'm sorry, I—"

Laura threw her arms around his waist, hugging him tightly, burying her face in his firm chest. She never wanted to let go of him. Why did their love have to be so complicated? She didn't want to lose him but there didn't seem to be any other way, not with a horrid fate staring her straight in the face.

Charlie hugged her back. "What is it, Laura?"

She began to cry. The words wouldn't come. She kept seeing him surrounded by other girls. She could feel him slipping out of her life.

He pushed her gently away from him, peering into her teary eyes. "Are you okay?"

She shook her head. "No."

"Laura! Tell me what's wrong!"

She hugged him again, thinking that she had to have faith in him. If he really loved her, he would understand. He *had* to understand.

Charlie stroked the back of her head. "Hey, I know. Let's go out tonight. Maybe a burger and a movie."

Laura drew back. "I can't, Charlie. Not tonight."

He grimaced again, shaking his head, turning away. "I can't take much more of this, Laura. Either you tell me what's wrong or I'm out of here."

"Charlie, please . . ."

He threw up his hands. "Why can't you tell me what's—"

A voice rose suddenly behind them, cutting through the noise of the hallway celebrations. "Hey, guys, how about it! Fourteen days of freedom. We finally made it."

Kimmy Anderson, Laura's best friend, moved up next to them. She smiled, not realizing Laura and Charlie were having a fight. Kimmy's short-cropped blond hair bobbed up and down as her head kept time to some inaudible beat.

"Par-tay," Kimmy went on, her blue eyes flashing. "We're ready to rock and roll. Just like the big kids."

Charlie's eyes were still locked on Laura's sad face. "Some of us are big kids, Kimmy. The rest of us want to stay in the sand box."

Laura's frown turned into an angry scowl. "That's not fair, Charlie. I told you—"

"That's right," he replied, "you told me. You told me all I need to know. Give me a call if you ever decide to grow up."

He started away from her, storming off down the hall.

Laura took one step after him. "Charlie, wait!"

Kimmy's smooth face turned bright red. She was a small pixie of a girl, cute, short and skinny. She had been best friends with Laura since the third grade. Kimmy felt terrible, thinking that she had somehow caused the fight.

"Laura, I . . ."

Laura sighed and wiped her eyes. "Oh, it's all right, Kimmy. It's not your fault."

"Ooohhh," Kimmy replied with a sudden glint of recognition in her blue eyes. "You told him."

Laura shook her head. "Worse. I *didn't* tell him. I couldn't find the words. They just wouldn't come out."

Kimmy sighed and shook her head. "Wow, he went ballistic over nothing?"

"Not really. I mean, it wasn't exactly over nothing."

Kimmy knew immediately what Laura was talking about. They had discussed it many times. Kimmy had often wished she had her own boyfriend problems, but she hadn't been so lucky—yet. She had been living vicariously through Laura, sometimes pretending that Charlie was *her* boyfriend.

"Maybe you should just tell him," Kimmy offered. "Get it over with. That might be best."

Laura spun around to open her locker. "Yeah, right. Then I've lost him for good."

"Oh, I don't know," Kimmy replied, straightening the folds of her wrap-around denim skirt. "I mean, hasn't Charlie always been a good guy? He's not like the others boys. He's sweet."

Laura stared into the mess of her locker. "I thought he was. Maybe he *is* just like the others. After one thing."

Kimmy leaned back against the lockers, gazing off dreamily into space. "I wish some guy was after anything I've got."

"What am I going to do, Kimmy?"

Kimmy shrugged, coming back to reality. "Tell him. Otherwise, you're going to blow it."

"What if I already have?"

"Then it doesn't matter," her best friend replied. "Just do it. What have you got to lose?"

"I don't know . . ."

"Do you love him?"

Laura nodded. "You know I do."

"Then tell him now, before it's too late."

Laura slammed the locker door. She didn't want anything in there. She wanted Charlie.

"You're right, Kimmy."

"I'm always right! Now go!"

Laura had to be with her boyfriend.

To give him the awful news.

Disaster.